Beijing Ding-a-Ling
Mao of the CIA

By George Arnold

Cover and Illustrations by Jason C. Eckhardt
Translations by Betty Cao

EAKIN PRESS ⚜ Fort Worth, Texas
www.EakinPress.com

This book is a work of fiction, completely the creation of the author's imagination. Locations and real figures are used in a fictional context. Any similarities to real characters or events contained in this manuscript are purely coincidental. However, the four cats of the CIA are real. They live with the author's family in Texas.

Copyright © 2015
By George Arnold
Published By Eakin Press
An Imprint of Wild Horse Media Group
P.O. Box 331779
Fort Worth, Texas 76163
1-817-344-7036
www.EakinPress.com
ALL RIGHTS RESERVED
1 2 3 4 5 6 7 8 9
ISBN-10: 1-68179-020-3
ISBN-13: 978-1-68179-020-6

Readers Talk About Beijing Ding-a-Ling

Students' Comments

- *"I love the two mischievous kittens, Luigi and Luisa. This book is enjoyable whenever I hear a story like, for example, the bell-dancing cat!"*
- *"I love how in each book you learn a little language from different countries. And now you learn Chinese! The idea that each character is a talking animal is so absurd it makes the book funny and entertaining."*

Comments from Parents and Grandparents

- *"The good guys win in the end. They always win. The fun part is discovering just how they do this."*
- *"Little kittens, working as a spy agency, going around the geographically-correct world learning about cultures and languages, while taking down bad guys is a little kid's dream and a grownup's fantasy."*
- *"What won't make readers hungry for both world knowledge and chocolate cake will make them feel like they're looking at China through the eyes of the bright, the fearless, and the adorable."*
- *"It's a delightfully funny book. I laughed at the chapter titles, and the character names were very imaginative. Children will love it!"*
- *"Enjoyable, easy read. The ending with the twins' cryptic conversation made me anxious to read the next book to find out what adventure they would be taking next."*
- *"I like the descriptions of the Forbidden City, Mao's Mausoleum, the information about money exchanges, and the cable cars up Victoria Peak in Hong Kong."*
- *"A detective story appealing to animal lovers of all ages. But being a kid helps."*
- *"I love these characters, and it's not hard to leave reality behind and get caught up in the latest capers of this lovable crew."*
- *"The dialog is wonderful and witty, and the story moves very well. Great addition to the collection."*
- *"What a delightful escape from reality. This latest episode in the lives of the cats of the CIA is creative, funny, and full of action."*
- *"Luigi and Luisa have once again made the perfect trap to catch bad guys causing world problems. Bravo, sweet kitties!"*
- *". . . a great yarn and proof that chocolate cake and ice cream help kittens be smart sleuths."*
- *"The neat thing about this book is parents and grandparents can also enjoy the story as they read to younger children."*
- *"The cultural differences between us and what we're used to in the United States are woven very well into a story that should intrigue any kid."*

*For my two smart and beautiful granddaughters:
Mariel Chun Shui and Julianne Li Ping*

Other books by George Arnold from Eakin Press

Cats of the CIA bilingual adventure series by George Arnold
for readers from eight to 108

Get Fred-X: The Cats of the C.I.A.
Hunt for Fred-X: Los Gatos of the C.I.A. – English/elementary Mexican Spanish
Fred-X Rising: I Gatti of the C.I.A. – English/elementary Italian
Tango With A Puma: Los Gatos of the C.I.A. – English/intermediate formal Spanish
Eiffel's Trifles and Troubles: Les Chats of the C.I.A. – English/elementary French
München Madness: Die Katzen of the C.I.A. – English/elementary German
Kremlin Kerfuffle: Koshki of the C.I.A. – English/elementary Russian
Beijing Ding-a-Ling: Mao of the C.I.A. – English/elementary Mandarin
COMING SOON: *Pharaohs' Follies: Kits of the CIA* – English/elementary Arabic

Detective Craig Rylander Clover-Mysteries
by George Arnold and Ken Squier

ENIGMA: *A Mystery*
UNDERCURRENTS: *The Van Pelt Enigma*
CONFLICTION: *A Moral Enigma*
ADVENTURES OF THE CHURCH-LADY GANG: *A Conspiracy of Crones*
FIRE AND ICE: *Beyond Alchemy* (by George Arnold)
COMING SOON: MULLIGAN: *Justice Reclaimed* (by George Arnold)

Nonfiction books for readers of all ages by George Arnold

Growing Up Simple: An Irreverent Look at Kids in the 1950s--Foreword by Liz Carpenter
Chick Magnates, Ayatollean Televangelist, & A Pig Farmer's Beef
BestSeller: Must-Read Author's Guide to Successfully Selling Your Book

For more information, visit the author's Website:
www.CIAcats.com
Or contact George Arnold at george@CIAcats.com

Contents

Author's Note	ix
Meet the Characters	xi
Introduction	xiii
Map of Beijing	xvi-xvii

PART ONE: A Big-Time Prickly Mission

1.	The Big Boss Man	2
2.	Flying High	9
3.	Four Hours to Tokyo	17
4.	Beijing Bound	23
5.	Making Tracks to Tiananmen Square	29

PART TWO: To Catch a Porcupine

6.	Stakeout	40
7.	Nowhere to be Found	45
8	Safely Hidden Away	53
9.	Laying Low . . . Hunting High and Low	60
10.	Truth or Jail	67
11.	Who's Going to the Hoosegow?	73

PART THREE: If at First You Don't Succeed

12.	Porcupine on the Lam	82
13.	A Sloth in Time	88
14.	The Chase is On	94
15	First Stop: The Forbidden City	100
16.	Double Trouble	107
17.	As the Sloth Turns	111
18.	The Usual Place	117
19.	A Fitting Finish	124

EPILOGUE—The Next Day	129
What's Next for the Cats of the CIA?	135
With Thanks to These	141
Glossary: Pronunciation Guide to Common Mandarin Words and Phrases	144
Other Books by the Author	155
Meet the Author	161

Author's Note

Mandarin is spoken daily by more people than any other language in the world. It is the official language of northern China, southwest China, Taiwan, and one of the four official languages of Singapore. For more than a billion people, it is their everyday language.

There are many variations in Mandarin, as in the other common languages of China and the world. Just as there are differences in spelling and pronunciation of the same English words when spoken or written in Great Britain and the United States, so are there the same differences in Mandarin among the various regions where it is spoken.

Mandarin has no alphabet, per se, and its pronunciation is governed by four levels of vocal tones: *level, rising, falling and high-rising*. These intonations of syllables and words help to make the spoken language mean what the speaker intends. Like English, the same series of consonants and vowels, i.e., syllables and words, may mean entirely different things. So the tone with which they are pronounced helps make clear what the words are intended to mean. In English, pear and pare sound alike, though one is a noun and the other a verb. In Mandarin, several words may be spelled exactly alike, but spoken with different tone levels to differentiate which is a noun, which is a verb, an adverb, an adjective . . . and its meaning in context.

In this book, we will attempt to provide basic pronunciation guides by using phonetics in the Roman alphabet. Please know that this method cannot be precise, but will rather provide directional sounds for the several hundred Mandarin words in the manuscript, accompanying tables, and the glossary at the end of the book.

It is my hope that this book—and others in the Cats of the CIA set—will increase interest among readers of all ages in the history, geography, cultures and lifestyles, and languages of the countries which each explores.

In my visits to these various countries around the world prior to writing each of the books, I found people much more alike than different. The same was true in China, where I spent more than three weeks traveling from Beijing to Hefei, to Guangzhou to Hong Kong. I found the everyday people of China to be friendly, extremely curious, and very interested in life in the U.S. In most all of the countries I've visited, I also found the people quite puzzled about our political system. In short, actions of the United States in many areas—domestic and foreign—made absolutely no sense to them. My feeble attempts to explain rarely cleared up their confusion. Yet we always had more in common than our differences. My hope is that these books will convey some of those commonalities and similarities to an audience ready to accept and embrace them.

George Arnold
Dallas/Fort Worth, Texas
2015

* x *

Meet the Characters
The Cats of the CIA (Cats In Action)

Buzzer Louis: Retired director of operations of Cats-In-Action (DO/CIA), called back into service from time to time to track down infamous international bad guys. Buzzer is a black-and-white tuxedo cat—and a calm, strategic thinker.

Dusty Louise: Buzzer's younger sister, a beautiful gray tabby. Dusty sometimes suffers from acute impatience, but she's working hard to overcome that flaw. She will not be completely happy until Luigi and Luisa behave as she thinks they should. Which will never happen.

Luigi: Extremely bright and hilariously funny tiny orange tabby, but all business when it comes to his work as an international detective.

Luisa: Luigi's twin sister, equally smart and wise beyond her months. Luisa and Luigi regularly concoct secret plans to see if they can make Dusty's eyeballs twitch.

Cincinnati the dancing pig: Buzzer's best friend and a contract operative to Cats In Action. Cincinnati is not only a skilled dancer and owner of 114 dance studios between Buffalo, New York, and Chicago, Illinois, but he also flies the Cats of the CIA around the world in his private jet, *The Flying Pig Machine*.

Socks: Appointed by the President of the U.S. to head the secret CIA organization, Socks mans their strategic operations center in the basement of the White House. There she oversees spy satellites and a variety of electronic eavesdropping equipment.

Keepers of International Secrets

POTUS: The President of the United States of America.

PPROC: President of the Peoples' Republic of China, Hu Jintao

Minister of Justice of the PRC—Wu Aying

Minister of State Security of PRC—Geng Huichang

Assistant Minister of Porcupine-Catching—No Quil, a large black cat

The Bad-News Villains

Ling Ting Tong: A multi-lingual and portly porcupine who is the real brains behind an international opium-smuggling ring. Mr. Ling must be stopped. But catching him is a prickly problem.

Elwood: Mr. Ling's sidekick. A not-too-bright, but very loyal, sloth. Known to his friends as "Flash."

No Way: Curator of the Mao Zedong Mausoleum and cousin to No Quil, assistant minister of porcupine catching. A black cat with four white feet.

Mysterious Woman: Works in the office of No Way. Lurks in the background, listening stealthily. Is she with the porcupine's team? Or not?

Ar-Chee: Big panda bear and titular head of the drug smuggling ring. Captured last week in Moscow by the Cats of the CIA and returned to China where he awaits trial in Qincheng Prison, just outside Beijing.

Introduction

Andrews Air Force Base—Near Washington, D.C.

The Flying Pig Machine's trip from Moscow's Domodedovo Airport to Washington, D.C. had been uneventful, but long. Fighting headwinds, Cincinnati the dancing pig and his co-pilot in training, Dusty Louise, had decided to stop twice for refueling in Iceland and in Canada, making what could have been a 15-hour flight last almost 20 hours. Using the autopilot, Cincinnati and Dusty had swapped command of the ship, one in charge while the other slept for a few hours at a time. Still, both were tired when they finally touched down at Andrews at 8:30 p.m. on a Friday night.

The other three passengers, Buzzer Louis, retired director of operations of the CIA—Cats In Action--and his and Dusty's tiny orange tabby twin siblings, Luigi and Luisa, had slept most of the way. They were all returning from three days in Moscow where they had captured the infamous international drug-smuggling panda from Beijing, Ar-Chee. With the help of the Russian Federation's Federal Security Service, known worldwide as the FSB, successor to the old KGB.

While Luigi and Luisa's plan to capture the panda had worked almost flawlessly, Ar-Chee's sidekick and translator, a portly porcupine named Ling Ting Tong, had escaped and was presumed to be heading back to China. Turns out, after opening the files in the porcupine's abandoned laptop computer, it was Ling Ting Tong who was the brains behind the smuggling operation. Capturing Ar-Chee had been a good step, but they all now feared that the smuggling operation would go on, not missing the panda's leadership very much.

To complicate the team's lives a bit more, Socks, their gray tabby boss who ran the CIA from her office in the basement of the White House, had called just before takeoff in Moscow to tell them the President of the United States wanted to see them as soon as they could make it to Washington.

They knew that meant there would be no trip home to Buzzer's ranch in the Texas Hill Country or to Cincinnati's base of operating his 114 dance studios from his home in Ohio. No, they would come to Washington like they were commanded. And the President would likely have another immediate assignment for them. Probably tracking down the porcupine.

That meant China.

While the tiny twins thought that idea to be a great adventure, Buzzer reminded himself that he had retired last year, and both Cincinnati and Dusty were tired from so many hours in the air piloting Cincinnati's twin fanjet Sabreliner. It was a small, but quite nice, business jet with a range of about 6,000 miles. Thanks to a long distance pack the dancing pig had ordered when the plane had been refurbished last year in Arkansas.

All that aside, when they touched down at Andrews Air Force Base, they found a caravan of three government vehicles waiting for them. Two black SUVs carrying Secret Service agents would precede and follow a bulletproof Cadillac limousine driven by a Marine Lance Corporal in full dress uniform . . . and carrying one other passenger, Socks. The Marine driver had been ordered to speak to nobody but Socks, and only if she spoke first to him. He was also to quickly forget anything he might hear any of his six passengers say. He thought, *This is top secret stuff, but it's going to feel a little like Noah's ark in here.*

As they deplaned in a closed hangar, Socks greeted them. "Good job on the panda. Good plan. Boris Alexandrovich, head of Russia's FSB, tells me Ar-Chee is on his way back to Beijing, in chains. Matter of fact, he's probably landing there just about now."

Luigi couldn't contain his curiosity. As they all climbed in the limousine for the trip to the city, he asked, "What does the president want with us? It's pretty late. Will he see us in the morning?"

Luigi was hoping to be rushed to their usual hotel, where

✱ Introduction ✱

he often saw important Senators and cabinet members, but preferred to spot major league baseball teams in town for a game or two with the local Washington Nationals.

"No, Luigi, the president wants to see all of us at once—tonight," Socks said. "He's been on the phone with President Putin of Russia, with the prime minister of Britain, and the premier of China this afternoon. All of them think the time to go after Ling Ting Tong is now, not later."

Cincinnati said, "Then he's going to need to assign a couple of pilots to us because neither Dusty nor I can face another long flight without some real rest."

Dusty looked startled. She said, "Cincinnati, you would let some stranger fly your plane?"

'Not my plane," the dancing pig said. "Somebody else's plane, maybe. One that's faster—if we're going to turn right around and head for China. That's a long flight. We'd have to refuel in Alaska and then again in either Japan or Korea. Figure a full 24 hours from here to there."

"I think the president has a better plan. But I'll let him tell you what he has in mind," Socks said as the three-vehicle caravan wound its way from Maryland to the heart of the capital and 1600 Pennsylvania Avenue—the White House.

"I'm ready to listen to his plan," Luigi said, adding, "As long as he has some chocolate cake and ice cream for Luisa and me."

Does the president have a plan already? Will he send the secret Cats of the CIA to China? Does he want them to capture the portly porcupine, Ling Ting Tong? Will they go in Cincinnati the dancing pig's airplane, The Flying Pig Machine? Or will they go in a faster plane with different pilots? Most important, will the president have chocolate cake and ice cream for Luigi and Luisa at the White House later tonight?

BEIJING

BEIJING NORTH TRAIN STATION

④

⑤

N W E S

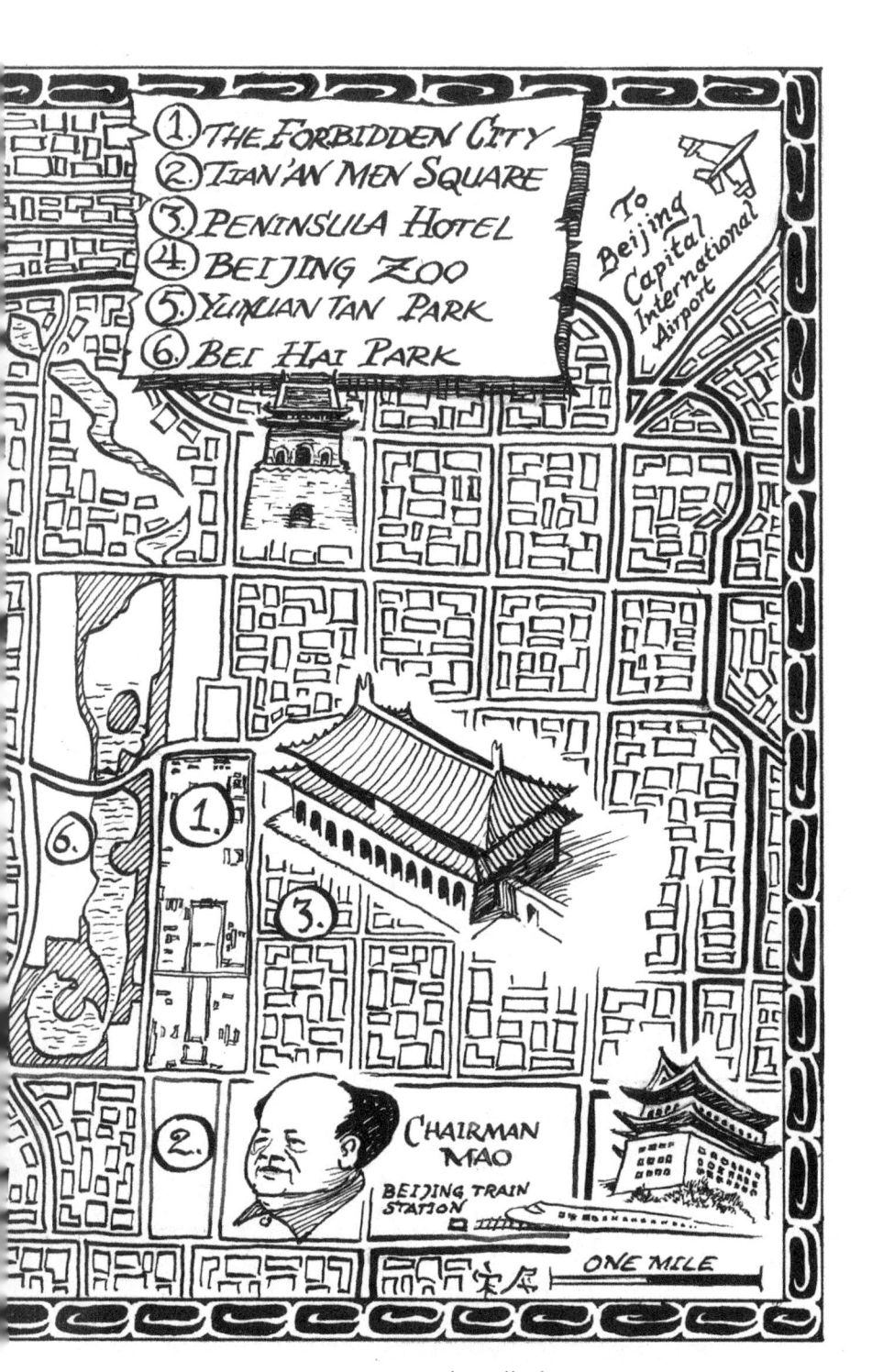

Part One
A Big-Time Prickly Mission

Chapter One
The Big Boss Man
Washington, D.C.
Andrews Air Force Base—Late Friday Night

A Marine corporal in full-dress uniform picked up the Cats of the CIA after Cincinnati the dancing pig landed his twin-fan-jet Sabreliner at Andrews Air Force Base. The corporal, driving a Cadillac limousine and accompanied by the head of Cats in Action, Socks, drove them straight toward the White House where POTUS, the president of the United States, waited for them.

The Marine driver had been told to forget any conversation he might hear, though he had not been told his passengers would include Buzzer Louis, a black-and-white tuxedo cat and former head of operations at the CIA—Cats In Action. He had brought the gray tabby Socks to meet the party, so he knew she was important and worked in the White House. But that's all he knew. He hadn't expected to be ferrying around not just Socks and Buzzer, but also the tiny and lively orange tabby twins, Luigi and Luisa, and the tired, but spritely, dancing pig, Cincinnati, and Buzzer's gray-tabby sister, Dusty Louise.

Neither did he know that Cincinnati's plane had just landed after a 20-hour flight from Moscow, forced by strong headwinds to make fuel stops in both Iceland and Canada along the way.

What he did know were two things: his passengers obviously were some kind of secret agents, and their operations were equally obviously top-secret; and he would have to work hard to forget the conversations coming from the back seat of his limo. He concentrated on the tail lights of the black SUV in front of him and the headlights of its twin following closely behind. Yes, these passengers merited not just a limo ride to the White House, but

★ The Boss Man ★

also a two-bulletproof –SUV escort.

They must be big-time VIPs, he thought. Way above my pay grade.

As he crossed the Maryland state line into the nation's capital, the chatter from behind him became even more animated. Most of it seemed to be coming from the tiny twin kittens, whom he'd only been told were named Luigi and Luisa.

Luigi was speaking. "So what's the big boss man want with us so urgently?" he said.

Luisa gave him a sharp look. "He's the president of the United States, Luigi. The most powerful man in the world. Don't be calling him big boss man."

"Well, that's what he is," Luigi retorted. "And he's got something up his sleeve that's mighty important if he wants to see us right away. Cincinnati's tired from the long flight. So's our sister, Dusty Louise. It can't be easy to fly that plane so far for so long. Look at them. They're half comatose."

Dusty's eyelids flicked up. She'd been listening. "The big boss man, as you so crudely called him, Luigi, is very busy, too. Obviously he needs us to take care of another international problem right away . . . or he wouldn't be rushing us to the White House so late at night."

Cincinnati simply nodded his agreement. Tired was not a strong enough description to tell how he felt at the moment. But always the trouper, Cincinnati would "make the scene," as he liked to say about going to important meetings.

Buzzer Louis looked at the twins and said, matter of factly, "I expect you two to behave like the successful international detectives you've become. No monkey business at the White House."

Luisa looked at her tiny brother. "Buzzer must be really tired. He's sounding just like Dusty Louise."

Luigi stood on the seat and saluted Buzzer. It was something he often did when he was about to say something he thought very important. "Don't you worry about Luisa and me, big brother. We're cool. And we'll be even cooler if our man POTUS remembers to have chocolate cake and ice cream for us. Right, Luisa?"

Luisa nodded her agreement just as the lead SUV pulled up to the gates in front of the White House.

* Beijing Ding-a-Ling: Mao of the CIA *

Their driver spoke softly into a small microphone. "We're at the White House. It has been my honor to drive you here tonight. I will be standing by to take you wherever you need to go after your meeting. One of my fellow Marines or someone from the Secret Service detail will escort you to meet with the president."

With that, he pulled the big limo to a stop, hopped out and opened a rear door for the group to exit. As Luigi climbed out, he shot the driver an enthusiastic salute, causing the driver to come instantly to attention, click the heels of his shiny shoes together, and return the kitten's salute.

Luigi smiled. The Marine smiled back, without thinking. Then he returned to attention, staring straight ahead. *That little cat's pretty funny*, he thought. *Too bad I can never mention him to anyone. Ever.*

The Oval Office—White House

As Cincinnati and the five cats of the CIA stepped into the Oval Office, Luigi spotted it first—a three-layer chocolate cake and a big bowl of vanilla ice cream. He remembered his manners, though, and spoke first to POTUS. "Good evening, Mr. President. How nice of you to remember our favorite refreshments."

He should have left his comments at that, but Luigi was on a roll, and he was already feeling the sugar-high all that cake and ice cream would produce. So he added one more thought. "What big problem in the world can we solve for you tonight?"

Dusty, of course, became mortified, as she usually did when the twins got a bit too rambunctious. She scowled at Luigi just as the president broke into laughter.

POTUS said, "Well, Luigi, I do have another very special assignment for the five of you. But first, let's have some refreshments and let me thank you for track-

* 4 *

∗ The Boss Man ∗

ing down that opium-smuggling panda, Ar-Chee, in Moscow. President Putin said he tried to recruit the two of you kittens for his FSB, their Federal Security Service, but you turned him down. Is that right?"

Luisa answered, fearing what Luigi might say next. And POTUS began dishing up bowls of ice cream and slices of chocolate cake for everyone. "President Putin was very nice to us, Sir," she said. "And he wanted to know if we might join his team. But we're on your team, Mr. President."

Luigi interrupted between bites of cake., "So we told him to find his own very clever kitten detectives . . . if he thought he could do that in Russia, that is."

POTUS shot a quick glance at Buzzer Louis as if to say, *Can you rescue me from these two enthusiastic kittens so we can get down to business?*

Catching the cue, Buzzer stepped forward. "Mr. President, what do you have in mind for our next assignment?"

POTUS looked around the group and said, "I'll bet you can guess what's up next."

He turned to Cincinnati the dancing pig who—so far—had ignored his cake and ice cream. *So as not to look like too much of a pig, he thought.* "I suspect we have unfinished work now in China, Sir. Beijing, if my guess is right," Cincinnati said. "We now know that Ar-Chee's sidekick and brains, Ling Ting Tong, has most likely gone back home to China."

"Correct," POTUS said. "But tell me about this porcupine. What do we know about him?"

To Dusty Louise's dismay, Buzzer looked to the twins. "You two probably know more about him than anybody. Tell the president what you know so far."

Luigi, still smarting from the look Dusty had given him the last time he'd spoken, pointed to his tiny twin sister, Luisa, and simply said, "Go!"

Luisa began, "Sir, as you said, Mr. Ling—that's Ling Ting Tong—in China they put their last names first. Mr. Ling, is a porcupine, and he's kind of fat."

Luigi interrupted, "We call him portly." Then smiled.

Luisa continued. "From the laptop computer he tossed in the trash in Moscow while we were chasing him, we learned that Mr. Ling is the real brains behind Ar-Chee's smuggling operation. You see, Sir, we learned that Ar-Chee the panda is a few ice cubes short of a glacier."

Again, Luigi interjected. "Really, to be fair, he's stupid, Sir. But he's in jail in Beijing now. The porcupine's the one we have to shut down. Or the smuggling will just go on."

The kittens began to appear to be a tag-team, taking turns answering the president's questions seamlessly, without missing a beat. Luisa added, "We do know he speaks many languages . . . he's multi-lingual."

"But then, again, so are we, Sir," Luigi said. "I expect we can speak as many languages as he can."

"But he does have one advantage over us, Sir," Luisa said.

POTUS looked interested and said, "And what's that, Luisa?"

"He can shoot his quills at us. And when they stick you, it really hurts."

"So we're going to have to sneak up on him and trap him," Luigi added. "I'm not wanting to get shot by one of those quills. Our ranch manager, Dr. Buford Lewis, once got 56 quills in his face. He hasn't been quite the same since."

Cincinnati stepped in to finish off the description of Ling Ting Tong. "That's about all we know at this point. Except . . . we were able to get Ar-Chee, who we'd stuffed into a gunny sack while the twins wrapped it with duct tape . . . we got him to admit he'd ordered Ling Ting Tong back to Beijing. The porcupine is supposed to meet him Sunday at noon by Mao's tomb in Tiananmen Square. Given the time differences that's still 30 hours away, and it's already Saturday morning in Beijing. Too bad we can't get there that fast."

"Why can't you?" POTUS asked, a grin on his face.

Dusty Louise answered, "To fly that far would take at least 16 to 18 hours in the air from here, Sir. Plus we would have to stop at least twice for fuel. Cincinnati's the pilot. And I can fly the plane, too. But, Sir, we just finished a 20-hour trip from Moscow to here, and both of us are really tired. To try it wouldn't be safe."

* The Boss Man *

"What if I could get you a faster plane? And someone else to fly it? Maybe a plane that can go more than 2,000 miles per hour and get you to say, Japan, by six o'clock Saturday evening? There we could have a regular airplane to take you from Tokyo to Beijing. And you could be in Tiananmen Square two hours before noon? How would that be?"

Luigi leaped up and saluted. "You're talking about the Blackbird, right? It's faster than a speeding bullet!"

"Here's the deal," the president said. "You finish up your cake and ice cream, then all take a nap in the Lincoln Bedroom. The driver who brought you here? He'll take you back to Andrews Air Force base in four hours. From there you'll fly straight to Tokyo in the SR-71 Blackbird—the plane Luigi mentioned and one some of you've flown in before. You'll then catch a ride on one of the State Department's smaller jets—an overnight flight to Beijing. You can sleep all the way. And be ready to capture Ling Ting Tong by noon Sunday. In China."

Not waiting for anyone else to answer, Luigi shouted, We're in!"

Do you think there's rally an airplane that can go more than 2,000 miles per-hour? Will it get our porcupine-chasing cats and Cincinnati to Tokyo in time to get on to Tiananmen Square before noon China time? Will Cincinnati fly it? Or Dusty? Will our special agents have enough time to sleep so they won't be tired when they get to Beijing?

Most important, will all the cake and ice cream Luigi and Luisa have just eaten give them such a sugar-high that they won't be able to sleep?

* Beijing Ding-a-Ling: Mao of the CIA *

让我们来学习一些普通话[1]

By Luigi and Luisa

Dusty Louise doesn't know yet that we both know how to speak Mandarin. We're not going to tell her until we have to. So please don't give us away. Meantime, here are some numbers for you to see how Mandarin works.

English	Mandarin	Say it Like This
One	一	Yi-
Two	二	Er\
Three	三	San-
Four	四	Si\
Five	五	Wu^
Six	六	Liu\
Seven	七	Qi-
Eight	八	Ba-
Nine Ten	九/十	Jiu^/ shi/
Twenty	二十	Er \ shi /
Thirty	三十	San- shi/
Forty	四十	Si\ shi/
Fifty	五十	Wu^ shi/
Sixty	六十	Liu\ shi/
Seventy	七十	Qi- shi/

(1) Let's Learn to Speak Some Mandarin

Chapter Two
Flying High
The White House—Late Friday Night

While Buzzer Louis, Dusty Louise and Cincinnati the dancing pig slept for four hours in the White House, Luigi and Luisa, high on sugar, prowled the big mansion with a friendly Secret Service agent named Cynthia. She took them to their preferred destination, the big house's kitchen, where they again dug into leftover chocolate cake and ice cream.

At about 2 a.m., Luigi said, "We'd better get back in bed before Dusty wakes up and catches us not sleeping."

Luisa said, "Right, but can we have just a little more ice cream first? And then I have a better idea. What if we got on the internet to learn about Beijing and Tiananmen Square? That way, we'll be three steps ahead of Dusty. One more time."

"Great idea," Luigi said. "But you know she's not going to like it. She never likes it when we know something she doesn't."

"Yes," Luisa said. "Just wait until she finds out we can already speak Mandarin. It's going to be an ugly scene. One more time."

So, with the help of Cynthia the Secret Service agent, the two tiny kittens found their way to the Cabinet Room, where they set to work on one of the White House's computers gathering information about China, Beijing and Tiananmen Square.

Andrews Air Force Base Outside Washington, D.C. 4 a.m.—Saturday Morning

Their limousine, with the same driver and the same two escorting SUVs, pulled up to a dark hanger on the northeast side of the big airfield. The only light came from a small bulb over a single door to the side of the closed hangar. Two men from each of the black SUVs led them toward the light. Luigi, of course, saluted their driver, and Luisa thanked him for both their rides. The door led to an office where one person sat at a desk studying charts on an oversized laptop computer.

As they came in the man stood and said, "Well, well, well. It's you again. And I see you've brought along a couple of stowaway kittens this time."

"Hello, Colonel," Cincinnati said.

Seeing that Luigi and Luisa seemed confused, Cincinnati explained to them, "This is the Air Force colonel who flew us from Munich to the Brazilian rain forest. Remember? The two of you had been kidnapped by Carlos the puma, and he had you in his private plane?"

The pilot was, in fact, the same person who had flown Cincinnati, Dusty and Buzzer to beat Carlos the puma's plane to Brazil, where they had captured the dangerous puma and saved the kittens from their kidnapper.

Luigi spoke right up. "Good to see you, Colonel. I'm the famous international detective Luigi Panettone Giaccomazza, and this is my sister, Luisa Manicotti Giaccomazza. We're legends in our own time. Do you have a name yet?"

The Colonel, dressed in what appeared to be some kind of pressurized flight suit, knelt down to speak to the kittens. "Glad to meet the both of you. I hear you trapped a rogue panda in the Moscow subways, and now you're after his sidekick? You're going to Japan with us, then? Is that where the bad guy's going to be? Or are you going on from there?"

Luigi saluted. "Need to know, Colonel. And you don't. Need to know, that is. But if you'll tell us your name, I might give you a hint."

"Sorry, Luigi. Need to know. And you don't." Standing again, he said, "Are we all ready to get underway?"

Once again, Luigi spoke up. By now, Dusty's eyeballs had begun to twitch. She wished Luigi would keep quiet. But she dared not tell him so because she knew Buzzer would want Luigi to say whatever he had on his mind. It seemed Buzzer had come to have great respect for the two kittens and their crime-fighting savvy. But Dusty still thought of them as babies. Babies who talked too much.

Luigi said, "You're not suggesting we leave without a briefing, are you, Colonel?"

Cincinnati broke into a big smile. He had taught the kittens the importance of preparing carefully before big flights, and he could tell Luigi and Luisa, who had never flown in the secret spy-plane, the SR-71 Blackbird, did not think themselves properly prepared.

The Colonel said to the kittens. "Okay, a briefing it is. What would you like to know?"

"Just the basics will do, Sir," Luigi said. "A rundown of the aircraft, its performance abilities, and a sketch of the flight plan."

The Colonel began. "As you already know, you will be flying from here to outside Tokyo in a top-secret aircraft. It's called the SR-71 Blackbird. It was manufactured almost fifty years ago in California by Lockheed. And it was used for many years as a super-high-flying spy plane—until satellite technology made it obsolete for that purpose. There are only two of them left, and they're kept under wraps at a location I'm not allowed to tell you about."

He turned and pointed to a door that led into the hangar. "One of them is sitting in there waiting to take you to Japan. I'll be your driver. Or pilot."

He led the group into the dimly lit hangar where they saw the Blackbird. "It looks a bit like a stork, doesn't it?" he said.

Luigi and Luisa agreed with that description. The colonel continued, "The plane is all black so as not to be so easily seen," the colonel said. "And, as you can see, it sits way off the ground on those spindly-looking landing gears. We will be leaving here in about 15 minutes. The first thing we'll do is refuel in the air over West Virginia."

"Why not just fill it up here?" Luisa asked an obvious question.

"Because, Luisa, this plane flies so high that its fuel tanks simply leak when it's on the ground. The more fuel we put in down here, the faster it will leak out. Scientists haven't been able to

* Beijing Ding-a-Ling: Mao of the CIA *

overcome that problem yet, so we do what we have to do—take off with not too much fuel and hook up with a tanker right away to fill us up to about 85,000 pounds of fuel. Then we climb up real high to more than 80,000 feet. Up there the air's thin enough that we can go pretty fast."

"How fast and how high?" Luigi blurted out. He was taking this briefing seriously.

The colonel, obviously enjoying the little kittens' curiosity, answered, "We'll pop along at about 2,200 miles per hour or so, Luigi. And we'll be about sixteen miles above the earth—at 85,000 feet."

Luisa's eyes opened widely. "So we're only about four hours from Japan?" she said.

"Give or take a few minutes, that's right, Luisa." The colonel said. "We'll have to come down to about 30,000 feet twice along the way for more fuel. That takes a few extra minutes each time."

Luigi had been doing some mental arithmetic. "This thing's a real gas hog, huh? Eighty-five thousand pounds of fuel only gets us a third of the way to Japan. Takes at least 35 pounds to go a mile?"

The colonel looked surprised. "That's right, Luigi. But you figured that in your head? He looked to Buzzer and Dusty and said, "That's amazing."

Luisa spoke up. "Well, Luigi rounded a bit. It's actually closer to 34.6 pounds per mile," Luigi burst out laughing and gave Luisa two paws up. "Thank you, Sir," he said. "I'm ready to go now." He turned to Luisa and said, "Are you ready, too?" She nodded. "Then let's get on with it. Why are we just standing around?"

Luigi was now in a hurry. Once he understood the plan, it was time to go for it.

The colonel pointed to a rack on a wall behind the big

plane as two men rolled up a 20-foot ladder with a platform on top—the ladder they would use to climb into the Blackbird.

The colonel said, "There are your pressurized suits and helmets. Go ahead and slip into them while I make a final inspection. Then, off we go!"

The wall rack held five flight suits and helmets. One large, two medium, and two teeny-tiny for the kitten twins.

As they slipped into the suits, all the lights but one on the ladder to the cockpit went out. The big hangar door began to open slowly, unveiling a black night sky with millions of stars. A sky just waiting for the high-flying secret agents of the CIA.

Wow! Do you think you would like to ride on a plane that goes so high and so fast? From Washington, D. C. to Tokyo in just four hours? How about Luigi and Luisa? Do you think they'll have fun in the Blackbird? Or will going so fast make them sick? Where do you think the two secret spy planes are kept now that they're no longer used to take pictures from 16 miles high? And who is this mysterious Air Force colonel who will be their pilot? Why won't he tell them his name?

✳ Beijing Ding-a-Ling: Mao of the CIA ✳

让我们来学习一些普通话[1]

By Luigi and Luisa

So far we haven't had any reason to speak Mandarin. So Dusty Louise still doesn't know our secret. Don't tell. Not yet. But we want to share some more of the Mandarin language with you. Here are some colors.

English	Mandarin	Say it Like This
Black	黑色	Hei- se\
White	白色	Bai/ se\
Red	□色	Hong/ se\
Blue	□色	Lan/ se\
Yellow	□色	Huang / se\
Green	□色	Lv\ se\
Gold	金色	Jin- se\
Silver	□色	Yin/ se\
Pink	粉□色	Fen^ hong/ se\
Brown	棕色	Zong- se\
Purple	紫色	zi^ se\
Orange	橙□色	Cheng/ hong/ se\
Gray	灰色	Hui- se\
Tan	黝黑□色	You^ hei- fu-se\

(1) Let's Learn to Speak Some Mandarin

Chapter Three
Four Hours to Tokyo
Andrews Air Force Base—4:30 a.m.—Up, Up and Away!

The four cats and Cincinnati crammed themselves into a small navigator's chair behind the colonel, who sat in the pilot's seat. The space was so cramped that Luigi and Luisa each had to sit on one of Cincinnati's knees as a small tractor tugged the black SR-71 Blackbird into the darkness and onto a taxiway.

As the pilot started the engines, the six inside the plane completed a microphone check of the plane's intercom system to be sure they would be able to talk to one another during the flight. The colonel rolled the gawky-looking Blackbird to the end of a runway, stepped on the brakes and spooled up the engines to 95% power. With the lifting of his foot, the Blackbird accelerated at a pace that pressed Luigi and Luisa back into Cincinnati's stomach.

Suddenly they were airborne, shooting almost straight up into the darkness above Washington, D.C. As they climbed, their pilot spoke into the intercom. "We'll climb only to 30,000 feet at first and head toward West Virginia. When we get there in a few minutes, we'll meet up with a big tanker and take on a full load of fuel—85,000 pounds. Then we'll go on up toward the stars and level off at about 85,000 feet. Do not remove your helmets or disconnect your oxygen. We need to all remain in our pressurized suits until we get to Tokyo."

Luigi said, "How fast are we going now, Colonel?"

The pilot said, "We'll stay subsonic until our first filling station. About 650 knots Luigi. That's just under the sound barrier. After we take on fuel and get really high, we'll trip over 2,000 knots and ride that speed to our next filling station just south of

Anchorage in Alaska. That'll give us enough fuel to make it to Japan with a few pounds to spare."

"How many pounds?" Cincinnati asked.

"I don't want to frighten you, Cincinnati, but I expect to land with no more than 2,500 to 3,000 pounds. That way, we won't be leaking fuel all over the tarmac."

By now they had been in the air only a few minutes. The colonel reset the frequency on his radio and called to a fuel tanker that loomed up ahead of them several miles away. "Filling Station, this is Blackbird approaching your six o'clock at five miles and closing. Send out the nozzle."

"Roger, Blackbird, we have you on screen," came the reply from the flying gas station.

Luigi, Luisa and Buzzer watched as the Blackbird drew up behind the big tanker. Dusty Louise and Cincinnati had fallen asleep. A long hose unreeled from the tanker into the bright landing lights of the SR-71, and the colonel pulled the Blackbird closer and closer until he could connect the needle-like nose of the Blackbird to the hose with a thunk.

"We have contact," the colonel said to the tanker. "Feed us some juice."

Refueling took only a few minutes. When the Blackbird's tanks filled all the way, the hose from the tanker disconnected. The colonel thanked the tanker and then said into the intercom, "Hold your hats. We're going up."

With that, he made a wide, sweeping turn to the right away from the tanker and began to climb. It seemed to Luigi that they were going almost straight up. Once they reached 85,000 feet and three times the speed of sound, the flight became very calm. Luigi and Luisa, who had stayed up all night eating cake and ice cream in the White House kitchen, fell sound asleep.

After less than two hours of level flight, the colonel woke them up. "We're almost to Alaska," he said, "and we're going back down for another tank of fuel. Be sure you are strapped in tight. Luigi and Luisa, you haven't done this before, but don't be frightened. We're going down fast. But we're not going to crash."

With that, the pilot reduced power and turned the nose of the

Four Hours to Tokyo

Blackbird downward into a series of spirals that Luigi thought more fun than any of the rides at Mother Goose Land where they had visited a few months before on their way back to Texas from Italy. As their bodies strained against their seat straps, Luisa said, "If we weren't strapped in, we would just float around, wouldn't we?"

The colonel answered, "Yes, as fast as we're falling you could be weightless for a moment or two, as if you were in outer space."

Immediately Luigi wanted to unstrap and float, but Cincinnati held him tight. "You don't want to fly around and get in the colonel's way, Luigi," the dancing pig said, just as they slowed and leveled off behind another big tanker.

Refueling went quickly, and soon the Blackbird was streaking again toward Japan at more than 2,200 miles per hour. The colonel said, "Tokyo time is 14 hours ahead of Washington, D.C. We left a little before five a.m., so we'll arrive in Tokyo-- about 6:30 in the morning. That's just less than 7,000 miles in a tad over four hours, including two refuelings. I want to get this plane into a hangar before it gets too light this morning. Just as he said that, the first rays of an early morning sun appeared behind them. Then they disappeared.

"How can we see the sun for a moment and then go back into darkness?" Dusty said.

"Seems like it should be sundown, not sunup."

Luigi said, "I know. I know. We're outrunning the sun, right? The earth is rotating west to east, and we're moving faster going west than the earth's rotation. Is that right?"

Cincinnati spoke up, "Exactly, Luigi. This plane can go so fast that it's possible to arrive at a destination before we left where we came from. By local time, that is."

Dusty looked puzzled. Luigi said, "Don't worry about it, big sister. That's the way we physicists see it. And that's the way it is." Dusty decided, rather than question any further, to just go back to sleep.

* Beijing Ding-a-Ling: Mao of the CIA *

Yokota Air Base—West of Tokyo—6:40 a.m. Sunday Morning—Local Time

The Blackbird touched down lightly at Yakota Air Base west of Tokyo and rolled immediately into a waiting hangar. Doors closed behind it. The colonel said as they were leaving the plane and removing their pressurized suits, "This is a U.S. Air Force base, but it's also used for private passenger flights and as a terminal for freight coming into and leaving Japan."

Buzzer Louis looked at the time. "We have five hours to get to Beijing and onto Tiananmen Square – if we're going to be there by noon."

Cincinnati added, "It's a three-hour flight, so that will give us less than two hours to get from Beijing Capital International Airport to Tiananmen Square. We better get hopping."

A jeep was waiting to take the cats and Cincinnati to their plane to Beijing. They said goodbye to the colonel. Luigi saluted and said, "Thank you, Sir, for a very exciting experience. I hope we see you again soon."

The colonel returned Luigi's salute and said, "That, Luigi, would be my pleasure."

The driver who took them to their next plane said that the Gulfstream G-650 that would take them to Beijing is the fastest private jet available. "It has a top speed of 610 miles per hour," the driver said. "Where are you going?" he asked.

"Beijing," Cincinnati answered.

"Then you'll be there in less than three hours. Figure two and a half hours flat including landing pattern and ground time."

"Who does this plane belong to?" Luigi asked.

"The U.S. State Department," the driver answered. "It's based here, but is available to ambassadors and embassy staff in several countries, including Japan, South Korea, mainland China and Taiwan. They use it whenever they need to get from one place to another in a hurry."

Luigi said, "You think 610 miles per hour is a hurry? You haven't seen anything yet. We left Washington, D.C. just four hours ago."

"Sure you did," the driver said. "And I'm a 500-pound gorilla." He obviously didn't believe Luigi, who was in no mood to argue.

"Just get us to our plane, please," Luigi said politely. Dusty was afraid of what Luigi might say next, but Buzzer gave him two paws up for behaving himself and not arguing with the driver.

The Flight to Beijing

Their plane had no sooner taken off than Luigi and Luisa began their usual begging for Buzzer Louis to tell them a story. "Pleeeeze, Buzzer, tell us about how you and Cincinnati captured Carlos the Puma four years ago at the Sheraton Hotel in Buenos Aires."

"Yes, please, Buzzer. We can't remember that story."

Dusty spoke up. "Wouldn't you two rather see a tape about Beijing and learn something about Tiananmen Square. After all, we'll be there before you know it, and we have to capture that pesky porcupine, Ling Ting Tong."

"We've already studied all about it, Dusty," Luisa said. "What do you think we were doing last night at the White House while you were sleeping?"

Luigi jumped in. "Studying up, that's what we were doing." He paused, grinned at his tiny twin Luisa, and said to Dusty, "So ... what would you like to know?"

Dusty Louise doesn't like the kittens to know things she doesn't know. Do you think she'll be upset that they've already learned about Tiananmen Square? Will this second plane really go 610 miles per hour and get them 1,300 miles to Beijing in less than three hours? How will they get from Beijing Capital International Airport to Tiananmen Square? Will someone from the Chinese government help them capture Ling Ting Tong? And will the portly porcupine even be there?

* Beijing Ding-a-Ling: Mao of the CIA *

让我们来学习一些普通话[1]

By Luigi and Luisa

We haven't eaten anything since we left the White House in Washington, D.C. After we catch that porcupine, we're going to be really hungry. But if you're in China, how do you know how to say the names of some of your favorite foods? Here are a few for you to learn.

English	Mandarin	Say it Like This
Cake	蛋糕	Dan\ gao-
Ice cream	雪糕	Xue^ gao-
Bread	面包	Mian\ bao-
Milk	牛奶	Niu/ nai^
Butter	牛油	Niu/you/
Fish	□	Yu/
Meat	肉	Rou\
Pork	猪肉	Zhu- rou\
Noodles	面□	Mian\ tiao/
Soup	□	Tang-
Cereal	谷□物	Gu^ lei\ wu\
Donut	□□圈	tian/ tian/ quan-
Apples	苹果	Ping/ guo^
Oranges	橙子	Cheng/ zi^
Bananas	香蕉	Xiang- jiao-
Corn	玉米	Yu\ mi^
Lettuce	生菜	Sheng- cai\
Tomatoes	番茄	Fan- qie/
Chicken	□肉	Ji- rou\
Cookies	□干	Bing^ gang-
Orange juice	橙汁	Cheng/zhi-
Beans	豆	Dou\
Cucumbers	□瓜	qing-gua-
Carrots	胡□卜	Hu/ luo/ bo/
Sugar	糖	Tang/
Salt	□	Yan/
Pepper	胡椒	Hu /jiao-
Cream	奶酪	Nai^ lao\

(1) Let's Learn to Speak Some Mandarin

Chapter Four
Beijing Bound
In the Air Heading for Beijing

The State Department's new Gulfstream G-650 not only was fast, but also comfortable and plush. Buzzer said to Cincinnati, "You need to get you one of these. It's bigger, faster and more comfortable than *The Flying Pig Machine*."

"Well, yes, Buzzer," Cincinnati said, "but one like this costs almost $65 million dollars. I think I can live with my Sabreliner a bit longer. It's slower, but I don't have the cash to trade up."

Luigi said, "Maybe Cats In Action will buy one for you. I'll ask Socks. We need to call her anyway."

Luisa asked, "What time is it in Washington, D.C. You don't want to wake her up, do you?"

"It's just seven in the evening there. On Saturday night. Right, Buzzer?"

"Right. Go ahead and call her. Tell her where we are and when we expect to get to Tiananmen Square. And, Luigi, ask her who is meeting us at the airport in Beijing."

Luigi and Luisa stepped to the back of the cabin with Buzzer's satellite phone to make the call as a flight attendant offered the passengers a breakfast selection of rolls, marmalade, bacon and milk.

"We'll pass on the bacon, thank you" Cincinnati said. "I

don't like to think about eating one of my brethren."

"Dusty set aside a roll and a glass of milk each for the kittens so they could have some breakfast when they finished their call to Socks. The call hadn't taken long, and soon the twins returned and dug into their rolls and milk.

"What did Socks say?" Dusty Louise asked.

"She said 'Good luck and be safe,'" Luisa reported.

"Who is going to meet us at Beijing?" Buzzer asked. "Or are we on our own to get to Tiananmen Square?"

"Socks wasn't exactly sure who would be there, but whoever it is will have a sign that says *The Socks Party*," Luisa said.

"I hope it's in English or Spanish," Dusty said. "I can't read Mandarin."

Before Luisa could stop him, Luigi blurted out, "Not to worry, big sister, Luisa and I can read Mandarin. We'll tell you what it says."

Dusty looked suspiciously at the twins. "And just where did you two learn Mandarin? Is there any language you can't already speak?"

"Probably a few," Luigi said, realizing he'd let their secret slip out before he and Luisa had planned how to break the news to Dusty.

Luisa quickly added, 'Don't be mad at us, Dusty. We're just kittens. We don't have all the important things to do that you do. So we have more time to learn things." She turned to Luigi for support. "Right, Luigi?"

"That sounds good to me, Luisa," Luigi said. "Besides, why can't you just be proud of us instead of jealous, Dusty?"

"I'm not jealous, you two. But I am amazed at how fast you learn things." She paused a minute, smiled at them and added, "And I guess I am proud of you. Anyway, you will interpret for us correctly, won't you? No more tricking me like you did in the Moscow Zoo?"

"We promise," Luisa said, snickering with Luigi as they remembered translating a Moscow zookeeper's Russian into English, but changing it so that what Dusty asked them to say actually got her into trouble. "It was funny at the time," Luigi said.

"What about my new airplane?" Cincinnati asked, smiling. He knew that was a silly question.

"Socks said that might be a good idea, especially since we're spending so much time flying all over the place," Luigi said.

"She said she'd ask the president next time she sees him," Luisa answered.

Cincinnati seemed surprised. He hadn't thought about a new airplane. He really liked *The Flying Pig Machine*.

Their breakfasts finished and with still another hour left before they would reach Beijing, the twins began their normal begging for a story from Buzzer. "Tell us about when you captured that opium-smuggling Panda in Hong Kong," Luisa said. "We can't remember all of that story."

Buzzer lifted the kittens onto his lap and sat one on each knee. He began the story. "It was three years ago," he said, "and Socks had asked us to go to Hong Kong to check out the panda named Ar-Chee. At that time, nobody knew for sure what he was up to, but everyone knew it was no good, whatever it was.

"Cincinnati and I checked into the J.W. Marriott hotel where Ar-Chee had been spotted the day before. We pretended to be Italian shoe salesmen. Socks had told us everything she knew about Ar-Chee, which wasn't much. But she knew he had fairly poor eyesight. And he couldn't resist Middle-Eastern belly dancers.

"The next morning, sure enough, Ar-Chee went into the big breakfast buffet off the hotel's lobby where he filled his plate with kippered herring, smoked salmon and two waffles."

Luigi looked at Luisa and said, "This is where it gets good."

Buzzer continued the story. "So Cincinnati dressed up like a belly dancer. He is a dancing pig, remember. And we went down into the basement of the hotel where there are shops and restaurants and a subway stop. The subway goes to Kowloon. We had given the concierge at the breakfast buffet ten Hong Kong dollars and asked him to tell Ar-Chee about the famous belly dancer, Fatima Petite, who would be performing right away in the atrium by the downstairs shops.

"Sure enough, just as Cincinnati began dancing, Ar-Chee ap-

✻ Beijing Ding-a-Ling: Mao of the CIA ✻

peared and fixed his gaze on Cincinnati's dancing. I was hiding behind an open umbrella so Ar-Chee couldn't see me. The panda walked up closer and closer to Cincinnati as he danced. He wanted to put some money into Cincinnati's sash—kind of a reward for the great dancing."

"What happened then?" Luisa asked. As if she hadn't heard this story a dozen times before.

"Well, Luisa, a subway train pulled into the station and the passengers getting off distracted Ar-Chee. Suddenly he saw me, and he bolted for the open train door. He was going to try to escape on the subway to Kowloon. But Cincinnati was faster. He grabbed my umbrella and beat the panda onto the train just as the doors began to close. So Cincinnati and Ar-Chee both were on the train. I leaped toward the door and swiped my left paw into Ar-Chee's face. And it stuck there as the door closed on my arm. So there I was, hanging outside the door by my claw stuck in Ar-Chee's face as the train began moving."

"Did you and Cincinnati catch him?" Luigi asked. "You didn't fall off the train, did you?"

"No, Luigi. Good for me, Cincinnati thought fast. He poked the tip of the umbrella into Ar-Chee's back and whispered to him, "This is a poison dart, Ar-Chee. You make a move, and I'll push the spring. And you'll be one dead panda."

"And it worked?" Luisa said.

"Perfectly," Cincinnati, who had just wandered up, said. "The police met the subway at Kowloon. It's just a few minute's ride. And they took Ar-Chee away. But do you know what went with Ar-Chee to the Hong Kong jail?"

"What?" Luigi said.

"One of the claws from my left paw," Buzzer said, lifting the paw to show the kittens, for the fifteenth time, at least, that one of his claws was missing.

Luisa, satisfied at the conclusion of the story, said, "And that claw was still in his face when we caught him last week in Moscow."

"I guess he will always have Buzzer's claw in his face to remind him to behave himself," Luigi said. "And now he's back in

* Beijing Bound *

jail in Beijing, still with your claw in his face. Serves him right!" Luigi concluded as he stood and saluted.

Just then, the G-650 slowed and began to descend. The captain said, "We're beginning our descent into Beijing Capital International Airport. We should be on the ground in less than 15 minutes. I've been told to taxi to the private plane's terminal. Someone from the Chinese government will meet you, clear you through immigration and customs, and then take you wherever it is you're going. It's been our pleasure to deliver you to Beijing this morning. If you really are on a mission from the White House, I hope you will tell the President that we delivered you promptly and safely."

Luigi and Luisa peeped out a window as the plane touched down at the busiest airport in Asia and the second busiest airport in the whole world. They saw ultra-modern buildings—terminal after terminal—with planes from all over the world parked at gates and moving along taxiways.

As the plane rolled to a stop at a private plane terminal, Luigi couldn't resist tweaking Dusty one last time. "Don't worry, Dusty. Stay close to us and we'll read all the signs for you."

Who do you think will meet the Cats of the CIA and Cincinnati? Will it be someone high up in the Chinese government? Will the sign really say The Socks Party? And will they have any problems clearing through Immigration and Customs? How will they get to Tiananmen Square? The airport is far north of Beijing, and the Square is in the middle of the city. Will they get trapped in a traffic jam? And, most important, will that pesky porcupine, Ling Ting Tong, actually show up at noon?

* Beijing Ding-a-Ling: Mao of the CIA *

让我们来学习一些普通话[1]

By Luigi and Luisa

Well, here we are in this giant airport in Beijing with a little more than two hours to get to Tiananmen Square. We'll need to know a lot of words about transportation to get from here to there. Here are some we can use along the way.

English	Mandarin	Say it Like This
Airplane	口机	Fei- ji-
Airport	口机口	Fei- ji- chang^
Taxi	出租口	Chu- zu- che-
Bus	公交口	Gong-jiao-che-
Shuttle	穿梭巴士	Chuang-suo-ba-shi\
Train	火口	Huo^ che-
Car	小口口	Xiao^jiao\che-
Limousine	豪口房口	Hao/ hua/fang^che-
Bicycle	自行口	Zi\xing/ che-
Boat	船	Chuan/
Ship	口船	Lun/chuan/
Sidewalk	人行道	Ren/xing/ dao\
Walking	走路	Zou^ lu\
Rickshaw	人力口包口	Ren/li\huang/bao-che-

(1) Let's Learn to Speak Some Mandarin

Chapter Five
Making Tracks for Tiananmen Square
Private Planes' Terminal
Beijing Capital International Airport—10 a.m. Local Time

As their plane taxied to its gate, the co-pilot said, "I'll tell you a bit about this airport, if you're interested."

Luigi, of course, was very interested. So he shouted, "Tell us!"

The co-pilot went on, "There are three large terminals here at Asia's busiest airport and the second busiest airport in the world. The newest, Terminal 3, is the second largest airport terminal in the world at more than 10 million square feet. That's almost 250 acres all under one roof. It's second in size only to Terminal 3 in Dubai, which is 18 million square feet—or 420 acres.

"But we're not going to any of the three big terminals. We'll be deplaning at the original small terminal built in 1958. It's tiny and is reserved for government officials and VIC's—Very Important Cats. That's where you'll meet whomever it is who will take you into the city. By the way, it's 18.5 miles from the airport to the center of the city. But today is Sunday, so the traffic shouldn't be too bad."

As their plane rolled to a stop, the captain said, "I hope you've had a good flight, and I wish you good fortune in whatever it is you're here to do."

The terminal was, indeed, very small. And, sure enough, standing just inside they saw an all-black cat carrying the sign they were looking for. As they entered the doors, the black cat rushed up to them and said, "Hello, my name is No Quil," Seeing a perplexed look on Dusty's face, he switched to English. "I am the assistant minister of porcupine-catching, and I'm here to rush you to Tiananmen Square. Please introduce yourselves. Then we shall retrieve your luggage and rush you through Customs and Immigration. Do you prefer that we speak in English? Or Mandarin?"

Dusty Louise quickly said, "English, please."

Luisa added immediately, "That was our sister, Dusty Louise. I am Luisa, and my twin brother, Luigi, and I speak Mandarin. So we shall be glad to translate whenever you need us to do so. This big black-and-white tuxedo cat is Buzzer Louis, and our friend the dancing pig is called Cincinnati." She smiled at having made the introductions perfectly.

Luigi added, "Since you are the assistant minister of porcupine catching, I guess you know why we're here?"

No Quil said, "I have not been told of your mission. Just to take you at once to Tiananmen Square and to assist you in any way possible. Do you know why I was selected for this important assignment?"

Buzzer spoke up, not sure what Luigi might say next. "Mr. No, we are here to capture a renegade porcupine known as Ling Ting Tong. Mr. Ling is the mastermind behind an international opium-smuggling ring. Your president, Hu Jintao, has asked our president for help. So we are here to bring Mr. Ling to justice."

"I see," No Quil said. "It's a good thing that I'm along on this mission, then. Porcupines are my specialty. Catching them is my most important challenge."

Luigi said, "How many quills?"

No Quil answered, "What do you mean, Luigi?"

"I mean how many quills have you been stuck with so far?"

"Oh, many thousands, Luigi. Many thousands." No Quil looked sad as he recounted his quota of porcupine quills. "But my skills have improved, and I can promise you we will catch this Mr. Ling with very few punctures. Trust me."

Looking back across his shoulders, No Quil said, "Follow me, and we'll get through the paperwork quickly. My car is waiting outside."

Just as he had promised, the black-cat assistant minister of porcupine catching led them quickly through Immigration and Customs, flashing his official credentials as they moved to the head of each line. Soon they were back outside, where No Quil's car waited.

Luigi looked at a clock just before he walked outside. "It's 10:45 now," he said. "We must be to Tiananmen Square within an hour. Can we do that?"

No Quil answered, "We have to go 29 kilometers, a bit more than 18 miles. We should have no problems."

As they climbed into his official car, Luigi soon understood why the trip would be a quick one. Mr. No's car was a black Buick, a U.S. car made in China and the preferred vehicle for most of the members of the Chinese government. On each side of the front bumper flags straightened and fluttered in the wind as the car began to move toward Capital Airport Motorway.

"For good measure," No Quil said, "I have this." He reached onto the seat beside him and set a flashing red light on the dashboard. Other traffic moved quickly to the side, and his car soon was rolling faster toward the city than any of the other vehicles.

No Quil explained, "For official business, I am allowed to use the flags and red light. And I can assure you this assignment is most official. The orders came jointly from two of the most important officials in our government: Wu Aying, minister of justice and Geng Huichang, minister of people's security. When the two of them issue an order, the rest of us know we're about to do something very important."

He paused long enough to swerve around a large garbage truck, and then he continued. "This porcupine. This Mr. Ling, tell me about him. The more I can learn ahead of time, the more help I can be in your mission."

The twins looked at Buzzer. Instead of answering himself, Buzzer said, "Our little twins know more about Ling Ting Tong than any of the rest of us. So I'll ask them to tell you about our quarry . . . and why it's so important to capture him."

Luigi turned to Luisa and said simply, "Go!"

So Luisa began. "Ling Ting Tong has been the number two agent in an international opium-smuggling ring run by a Chinese panda known as Ar-Chee. You see, Mr. No, the two of them have been smuggling opium from the poppy fields of Afghanistan all across the Pacific rim. A couple of weeks ago, they traveled to Russia to try to enlist the Russian mafia as distributors for their drugs in Moscow. That's where we captured Ar-Chee just four days ago. The panda is now in jail here in Beijing after our friend Boris Alexandrovich, head of the FSB—Russia's Federal Security Service--and Vladimir Putin, president of the Russian Federation, had him deported back to his home country."

She paused, and then asked. "Are you with me so far? I'm getting to Ling Ting Tong now."

"I'm with you," No Quil said as he honked at a slow moving car that took a bit too long to get out of his way.

Luisa continued, "While we captured Ar-Chee in the Moscow Metro, their subway, by pretending to be Middle-Eastern belly dancers, Ling Ting Tong and the panda had split up. Mr. Ling took a different subway and escaped. We found his laptop in the trash in far northwest Moscow. From it we learned that Ar-Chee had expected to get away. And he had told Ling Ting Tong to meet him today at noon at the tomb of Mao Zedong[1] in Tiananmen Square.

"That's why we're headed there, and why we must be there before noon. Also, it may be helpful for you to know that Ling Ting Tong is not only portly, but also speaks many languages. He's smart. We learned from his laptop a couple of more things: One, he was clearly the brains behind the smuggling operation. And, two, he loves to shoot quills at cats. So that's our challenge. To surround him, capture him and not get quilled to death."

"Ah, yes," No Quil said. "A challenge I've faced many times in my official duties. Try not to worry, Luisa—and all of you. I have my ways of dealing with quill-shooters. And I shall protect you as much as possible."

He paused as the car slowed down on East Chang an Jie Street, right in front of Tiananmen Square. As the car stopped at the curb, he said, confidently, "We shall catch that porcupine, today—or soon. Or my name isn't No Quil. And I don't wish to be sent to retraining."

---

1. Mao Zedong led the Chinese revolution after World War II which established the People's Republic of China as a Communist country.

∗ Making Tracks for Tiananmen Square ∗

Luigi checked the time. It was 11:20. He said as they got out of the car, "We've got time."

"Let's case this joint."

Dusty Louise gasped.

But the assistant mister of porcupine catching laughed. He said, "I think I'm going to like you, Luigi. A lot."

Will the team have time to case the joint, as Luigi suggested, before noon? Will they be able to take up positions so that Ling Ting Tong doesn't see them until it's too late? What "ways" do you think No Quil will bring to the hunt to help them? And what did the assistant minister of porcupine catching mean by not wanting to be sent to retraining? Most important, will the wily Ling Ting Tong show up at noon? If he does, will he get away once again?

※ Beijing Ding-a-Ling: Mao of the CIA ※

让我们来学习一些普通话[1]

By Luigi and Luisa

Right now it's warm and sunny in Beijing. But what if you came here at another time of year? What would the weather be like? And how would you know how to describe it? Here are some weather words for you to learn so you're ready any time of year.

English	Mandarin	Say it Like This
Weather	天气	Tian- qi\
Temperature	温度	Wen- du\
Cloudy	多云	Duo- yun/
Stormy	暴风雨的	Bao\ feng- yu^ de
Rainy	多雨的	Duo- yu^de
Snowy	多雪的	Duo- xue^ de
Rain	下雨	Xia\ yu^
Snow	下雪	Xia\ xue^
Sleet	薄冰	Bo/ bing-
Hail	冰雹	Bin- bao/
Wind	风	Feng-
Sun	太阳	Tai\ yang/
Sunshine	阳光的	Yang/ guang- de
Moon	月亮	Yue\ liang\
Hot	热	Re\
Cold	冷	Leng.^
Dark	黑暗的	Hei- an\ de
Light	明亮的	Ming/ liang\ de

---

1. Let's Learn to Speak Some Mandarin

TIAN'AN M
1. MAO ZEDONG
2. GREAT HALL
3. MUSEUM
4. ZHENG

CHANG AN JIE STREET

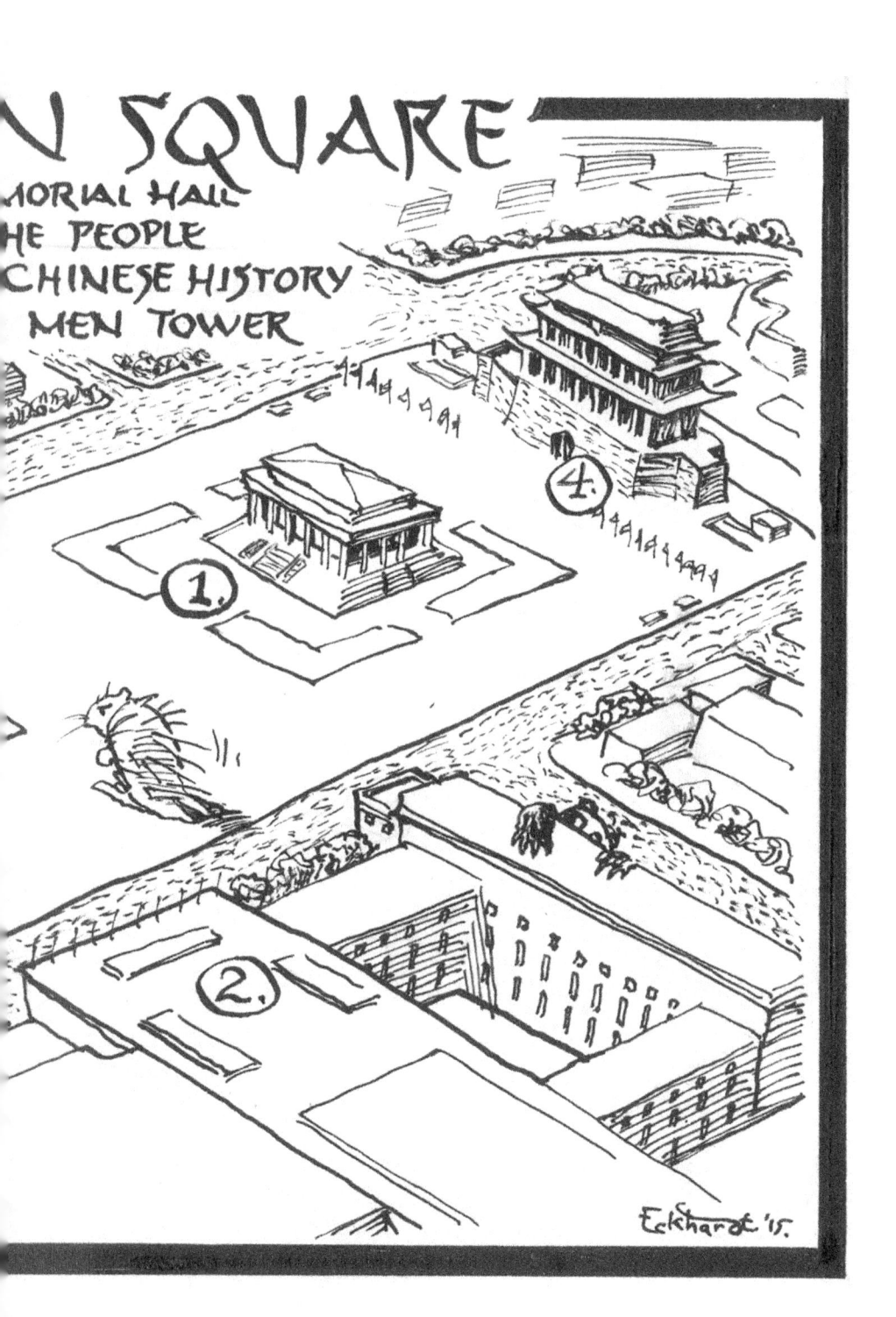

N SQUARE
 ORIAL HALL
 HE PEOPLE
 CHINESE HISTORY
 MEN TOWER

1.

4.

2.

Eckhardt '15.

Part Two
To Catch a Porcupine

Chapter Six
Stakeout

Tiananmen Square—11:45 a.m.

Luigi and Luisa crouched underneath the Monument to the People's Heroes right in the middle of what seemed to them a huge square. As they kept their eyes focused on the Mao Zedong Memorial Hall where Ling Ting Tong might show up in a few minutes, they were surrounded to their right by The Great Hall of the People, the seat of government for the country, and on their left by the Museum of Chinese History, one of the largest and most extensive museums in the world. Yet both these mammoth buildings sat more than 100 yards away from them. In opposite directions.

"This place is enormous," Luigi said, climbing up a couple of feet on the monument to better see over the crowds strolling from place to place.

Luisa answered, "Yes, Luigi, I would say it's at least 10 times as big as St. Mark's Square in Venice. Remember that place? Where Il Papa, the Pope, himself, gave us some ice cream?" She looked around and then said, "But where are all the pigeons? I don't see a single pigeon."

Knowing Ling Ting Tong would recognize Dusty Louise and himself from their encounter in Moscow a few days ago, Buzzer decided the best place for the two of them would be between where they had left No Quil's car at the curb of Chang an Jie Street and the entrance to the Square—on either side of the subway station. "If Ling Ting Tong comes by subway, we'll be the first to see him," Buzzer said.

Buzzer continued, "Cincinnati and No Quil will cover the front and back entrances to Mao's Mausoleum. And Luigi and

Luisa, down by the People's Heroes Monument, will see him if he comes through the Forbidden City. If he shows up, we can't miss him. We've got the place covered."

"Why didn't No Quil call in some reinforcements?" Dusty asked. "This place is so big we could use a few more sets of eyes."

Buzzer said, "You can see the place is crowded, Dusty. If there were to be a lot of uniforms scattered about, that might tip Ling Ting Tong off. The place needs to look like it's just a normal Sunday in the late summer so Mr. Ling won't get scared off."

As the two of them kept their eyes glued to the subway exit, Dusty asked, "What is that Forbidden City way down there behind where the twins are hiding? Why is it forbidden? And who's forbidden from going in there, anyway?"

"Dusty, the Forbidden City was built 700 years ago by more than a million workers to be the home of Chinese Emperors. And for the last 500 years, that's exactly what it was—the home of 24 emperors. Today it's called the *Gùgōng* in Mandarin. That means *Former Palace*."

"It looks pretty big. Who needs a palace that big, anyway?" Dusty said.

Buzzer said, "I don't suppose anybody needs one. But I heard it has almost 10,000 rooms. Seems like it would be easy to get lost in there."

"What about the *Forbidden* part. Who and what are forbidden?" Dusty persisted.

Buzzer said, "I don't know about that. We'll have to ask Luigi and Luisa. They seem to know everything about everything these days."

"They won't know, Buzzer. I'll bet you they won't know." Dusty was sure she had finally found something the twins wouldn't know. It seemed to her that anything she didn't know, they did know. This would be her chance to catch them without their usual facts.

As the clock moved right up to noon, Cincinnati and No Quil remained on high alert. They knew Ling Ting Tong was supposed to meet Ar-Chee, now in jail, at the building they had surrounded, but the information on the porcupine's laptop wasn't clear about which side of Mao's tomb. Or whether they were to meet inside or outside. The meeting place apparently was known only to the captured panda and the on-the-loose porcupine.

Cincinnati spoke into a small microphone clipped on his left ear. "Has anybody seen Mr. Ling yet?"

No Quil answered, "He hasn't gone through the front door yet. Unless he's already in there."

Buzzer said, "He hasn't come out of the subway, either. What about you, Luigi and Luisa? Have you seen him?"

"Not yet," Luigi said. "There are so many pedestrians milling around between us and Mao's tomb, that we won't be able to see him unless he passes right by us, I tried climbing up the monument to get a better view, but some kind of policeman said if I didn't get down, he would whack me with a baton."

Luisa spoke up. "We don't want any baton whacking. That might just be worse than taking a quill or three for the team."

Cincinnati said, "It's almost 12:15. If he's a punctual porcupine, he must be in Mao's Mausoleum already. He hasn't passed by the twins. He hasn't come out of the subway. And he hasn't gone in the front or back doors in the last half hour."

Buzzer said, "Mr. Ling is either in that building . . . or he somehow found out Ar-Chee was captured in Moscow and knows not to show up. But I wonder how that could have happened?"

"Natasha!" Luigi and Luisa shouted in unison. Luisa went on, "Natasha must have told him. I never trusted her."

"Who is Natasha?" No Quil asked.

Luigi answered, "Natasha was the first assistant to Boris Alexandrovich, the head of the Russian Federation's secret police, the Federal Security Service. Boris didn't trust her, and neither did we."

Luisa added, "She's supposed to be on her way to New York to become the social secretary to her father. He's the Russian ambassador to the United Nations. I'll bet she got a ton of Rubles from Ling Ting Tong for ratting us out."

"What does she look like?" No Quil asked.

Cincinnati said, "She's a rather striking—beautiful, I suppose—calico. She's gray and brown and orange with incredibly long eyelashes."

Dusty had to step in. Her jealousy wouldn't let her remain silent. "She's not that great looking. Besides, she's as crooked as Cincinnati's tail."

Buzzer, ever calm, said, "Natasha might have tipped Mr. Ling off. But we don't know that for sure. I think the best thing we can do right now is to all stroll quietly and separately into the Mausoleum and have a good look around. Cincinnati, you stay inside by the back door, and Mr. No, you cover the front door from inside. The rest of us will move around until we either spot him or know for sure he's not in there. Luigi, you check the men's rooms. Luisa, you check the ladies' rooms. Dusty and I will cover every inch inside there. First one to see him, say, 'Ling' into your microphone."

So the five cats and the dancing pig converged on Mao's tomb to scour it completely. If the pesky porcupine, Ling Ting Tong, should be in there, he would be found.

Do you think Ling Ting Tong will be inside Mao's Mausoleum? If he is, will our heroes be able to capture him and take him to jail? If he's not, do you think he might have been tipped off by the Russian agent Natasha? For a lot of Russian money? And what about the twins? Will they know why the former Palace area is called The Forbidden City? If they do, will Dusty Louise get upset? Or will she be proud of them? And, most important, if the pesky porcupine isn't in the Mausoleum, what will the Cats of the CIA, Cincinnati, and No Quil do next?

* Beijing Ding-a-Ling: Mao of the CIA *

让我们来学习一些普通话[1]

By Luigi and Luisa

So here we are at Tiananmen Square, one of the most famous places in all the world. If you were here, how would you say the names of the many sights and sites all around here? Here are some words to help you know how to say them correctly.

English	Mandarin	Say it Like This
Tiananmen Square	天安门广场	Tian- an- men/
Mao's Mausoleum	毛主席纪念堂	Mao/ zhu^xi/ ji\ nian\ tang/
Monument to the People's Heroes	人民英雄纪念碑	Ren/ min/ ying-xiong/ji\nian\bei-
Great Hall of the People	人民大会堂	Ren/ min/ da\hui/ tang/
Arrow Tower	箭塔	Jian\ ta^
Museum of Chinese History	中国历史博物馆	Zhong-guo/ li\shi^bo/ wu\ guang^
The Forbidden City	紫禁城	Zi^jin\ cheng/
Gate of Heavenly Peace	天安门	Tian- an- men/
Palace Museum	故宫博物馆	Gu\ gong- bo/ wu\guang^
Gate of Divine Might	神武门	Shen/ wu^ men/
Imperial Garden	御花园	Yu\ hua- yuan/
Jingshan Park	景山公园	Jing^ shan- gong- yuan/
24 Emperors	24 位帝王	er\ shi/ si\ wei\ di\wang/
Chang an Jie Street	长安街	Chang/ an- jie-

---

1. Let's Learn to Speak Some Mandarin

Chapter Seven
Nowhere to be Found
Tiananmen Square—Mao Zedong's Tomb

With one thought in mind—*find Ling Ting Tong*—the search team of six cats and one dancing pig dug through every nook and cranny in the building.

After one complete scouring, during which they found nothing, Luigi had an idea. He said to No Quil, "What if we had some kind of fake emergency and made everybody leave the building? Three of us could cover the front door, and the other three the back door. That way, if Mr. Ling is, by chance, still hiding in here, he'll have to leave. And if he leaves, we can't possibly miss him. What do you think? Huh?"

No Quil immediately checked a list on his cell phone. "As it happens, my cousin, No Way, is in charge of the building on Sundays. Like me, he is mostly black, but he has four white feet. Wait here. I'll go find him. Your idea's worth a try, Luigi."

As No Quil raced off and up a staircase, Luigi stood tall and saluted. "Chalk up one more good idea for the kittens. Right, Luisa?"

"Right!" his tiny twin sister said, giving Luigi two paws up.

Even before No Quil had returned, the lights inside flashed. Once, twice, three times. Immediately a voice came over the building's speaker system. "Attention! Attention! This building is suffering a problem with the lighting system. Please leave quietly by the nearest exit. Please leave now. We will have the problem fixed within a few minutes, and you may return then. Please leave the building. Now!"

Luigi, Luisa and Cincinnati raced to cover the front door while Buzzer, Dusty and No Quil, who had just gotten back to

* Beijing Ding-a-Ling: Mao of the CIA *

* 46 *

* Nowhere to Be Found *

the group, went to the back door. Slowly everyone inside the building began to leave. Out both doors poured dozens of visitors—cats, dogs, two monkeys, a giraffe in a wheelchair pushed by six hedgehogs, and assorted Chinese and foreign visitors to Tiananmen Square.

Within five minutes, the doors locked automatically. It appeared that the building had emptied of all those inside. Just to be sure, No Quil led Buzzer and Dusty to search the upper floors, while his cousin, No Way, led Cincinnati and the twins for one final search of the ground floor.

They all quickly discovered that every room, every hallway, every closet and even all the trash cans simply were empty. Nobody seemed to be left in the building.

No Way said to the group, "I must re-open this building at once. I have risked much by this short closing. So now I have to go to my office and make up some logical report about why I did it. I'm afraid porcupine hunting will not be an acceptable reason."

As he headed for the stairs, pressing a button to open the doors again, he said, "I wish you good luck. I hope you find this fiend. Soon."

And then he was gone.

Buzzer said, "It's time to sit down patiently and think this problem through. No Quil, is there a quiet place nearby where we might get something to eat and figure out what to do next?"

"Come this way," No Quil said. "It will be my pleasure to treat all of you to a Chinese Sunday lunch."

Back in the Now-Busy Mausoleum

As the Cats of the CIA, Cincinnati and No Quil left, headed toward The Forbidden City and one of No Quil's favorite restaurants, a small black panel hidden behind rows of potted flowers slowly opened. Ling Ting Tong peered out from beneath the glass-topped resting place of Mao, former revered leader of the People's Republic of China.

Mr. Ling thought, *That was not such a great hiding place, but it worked.* He slipped out through the flowers and joined the

* Beijing Ding-a-Ling: Mao of the CIA *

throngs of visitors milling around Mao's resting place. Now sure that his pursuers had left, he strolled from the back door to meet his accomplice, a slow-witted sloth named Elwood.

Elwood, whom Mr. Ling often described as "loyal to a fault, but dumb as a brass hammer," leaped to attention, filled with questions. "Where is Ar-Chee, our panda leader?" he asked. "And what took so long? Why did everybody leave the building for a few minutes and then all go back in? I'm confused."

"Yes, Elwood, you are confused. Maybe more than I am, but still what's happened is naturally confusing. We were here as Ar-Chee had asked, but he was either very late or he didn't come at all. Then, as I was sitting quietly waiting for him, I spotted those infernal cats and their pig friend lurking around. The same ones who were after Ar-Chee and me last week in Moscow. All I can guess is that they must have caught Ar-Chee and he must have been forced to tell them I would be here at noon today."

Elwood looked even more confused. "What does that mean, Mr. Ling? Are we in trouble now?"

"Good guess, Elwood. I'm sure that bunch is looking for me. They want to put us out of business. To end our very lucrative smuggling operation."

"We can't let that happen," Elwood said. Then, looking pained, he added, "Can we? What would we do if we didn't sell the opium from Afghanistan all over the place?" He scratched his head and added, "Where are all those places we sell it, Mr. Ling?"

"Never mind, Elwood. What it means is we either escape from them . . . or we end up in prison. For a long, long time."

Tears rolled down Elwood's cheeks, dropping either side of his long nose. "I'm afraid to go to prison. You might have to be smart to be in prison. I'm not real smart, you know. But I try hard."

"Yes, Elwood. You do try hard. And right now we have to just disappear for a while until those pests give up and go back to where they came from."

"Where did they come from, Mr. Ling? I bet it's a long way off."

"They came from the United States, sent here by their president. Or Vladimir Putin, president of the Russian Federation. Or even our own premier."

"Does our own premier not like us? Why not?" Elwood, ever more confused, found himself a tick shy of a total meltdown.

Ling Ting Tong said, "Try not to worry, Elwood. You do exactly as I tell you. And we'll hide so they can't find us. We'll hide right here in Beijing."

"Is this like hide-and-seek? I like to play that game." Elwood's mood brightened slightly.

"Elwood, don't think so much. You'll hurt your head. Come on. Let's make tracks."

As they walked away toward the subway next to Chang an Jie Street, Elwood looked back. He didn't see any tracks. And that worried him.

As the two entered the subway, Ling Ting Tong's brain was churning. *They caught Ar-Chee in Moscow because he isn't real smart. Smarter than Elwood, to be sure, but nowhere nearly as smart as I am. I will figure out how to keep from getting caught. Just as soon as we get back to our home. Only problem is that Elwood knows too much. But he's mostly harmless. I hope.*

Da San Yuan Restaurant—Next to The Forbidden City

As the porcupine chasers entered a large restaurant and found a table in a corner where they could talk quietly, No Quil said, "We could have just grabbed some snacks from some of the vendors in The Forbidden City, but I wanted to treat you, at least once, to one of the finest restaurants in Beijing."

They began to look at their menus. Dusty Louise said, "I don't see any rice dishes. I thought rice was eaten by almost everyone in China."

No Quil said, "Not so much in Beijing. Our city is far to the north where it gets very cold. Heavier, more substantial dishes like breads, noodles and dumplings are more common here. And of course, there is always the most famous dish in China, Peking duck. Would you like to try that? One duck is just right for six. And there are six of us."

Cincinnati studied the Peking duck on the menu. "No, thank you, No Quil. I see it's served in little pancakes with onions, cucumbers and turnips. When I was just a youngster, I had to eat turnips. Every day, turnips. I hope to never see another turnip—ever again."

"I understand," No Quil said. "Then each of you choose whatever looks good to you. And then we'll talk."

After much discussion and a little negotiation, the group settled on an array of different dumplings, Zhajiang noodles and steamed bread, served family style.

Luisa nudged Luigi. She said, "Remember when we were wondering why we didn't see any pigeons on Tiananmen Square? Well, here's why." She pointed to a listing on the menu. "They eat pigeons," she said. "That's why."

Luigi whispered, "Are there any buzzards on that menu?" He began a line-by-line search to see for himself.

While they waited for their order to be prepared, Dusty remembered her bet with Buzzer. She couldn't wait to ask the twins her question. Buzzer saw her fidgeting and said, "Go ahead, Dusty. Ask Luigi and Luisa your question."

Hearing their names mentioned, the twins perked up. They stared at Dusty. "What is it, big sister?" Luisa said. "How can we help you?"

Dusty said, "I don't think you can, but I'll give you a chance. When you can't answer, we'll let Mr. No tell us the real answer."

"Shoot," Luigi said," grinning at Luisa. He saw another chance to make one of Dusty's predictions fall apart.

"Okay," Dusty said. "Here are the questions: Why is The Forbidden City forbidden? And who is forbidden to go there?" She sat back, smug in her belief that the twins wouldn't have a clue.

To her surprise, Luisa said, "That's easy. Do you want to tell her, Luigi?"

Luigi stood and saluted. "Here's the deal," he said.

He went on, "Hundreds of years ago, ancient Chinese astronomers figured out, although they were wrong, of course, that one star was the center of the heavens. That star was Polaris, also known as the Purple Star. They thought that the Heavenly Emperor lived in a Purple Palace. So they called the palace for the emperor on earth the Purple City. Nobody could enter the Purple

※ Nowhere to Be Found ※

City without the permission of the emperor. So they called the place 'The Purple Forbidden City.' Since then, it's become known simply as the Forbidden City."

Luigi smiled, turned to No Quil and said, "Is that about right?"

"Exactly right, Luigi. You two have been studying up for this trip. I can see that."

Luisa spoke up. "So why did you think we wouldn't know that, Dusty? We told you we read all about Beijing and Tiananmen Square while the rest of you slept in the White House."

Dusty, once again defeated by the twins' extraordinary grasp of seemingly almost everything, just smiled. "I'm very pound of both of you," she said. And she winked at Buzzer, who thoroughly enjoyed winning his little bet with his sister.

Why do you think our porcupine-catching team missed finding Ling Ting Tong in Mao Zedong's Mausoleum? Do you think he slipped in before they got there and hid when he saw them? Does Ling Ting Tong know for sure what happened to Ar-Chee? And what about this sloth, Elwood? He doesn't seem too bright. Do you think it's possible he might slip up and give away how to find Mr. Ling? What do you think the Cats of the CIA, Cincinnati and Mr. No will do next? Beijing is a big city with more than 14 million residents. How will they go about tracking down one porcupine? Finally, would you eat Peking duck? With or without turnips?

✷ Beijing Ding-a-Ling: Mao of the CIA ✷

让我们来学习一些普通话[1]

By Luigi and Luisa

No Quil will pay for our fine meal at the restaurant where we've just eaten. But soon, we will have to begin paying our own way. So we'll need to know some words about money. Here are some words to help you when you come to China.

English	Mandarin	Say it Like This
Money exchange	外币兑换	Wai\ bi\ dui\ huan\
Bank	银行	Yin/ hang/
Money	钱	Qian/
Traveler's checks	旅行支票	Lv^ xing/ zhi- piao\
Exchange rate	汇率	Hui\ lv\
Dollars	美金	Mei^ jin-
Yuan Renminbi[2]	人民币	Ren/ min/ bi\
Coins	硬币	Ying\ bi\
Cost	成本	Cheng/ ben^
Price	价格	Jia\ ge/
Change	找零	Zhao^ ling/
Credit card	信用卡	Xin\ yong\ ka^
Discover	发现卡	Fa- xian\ ka^
Visa	唯萨卡	Wei/ sa\ ka^
MasterCard	万事达卡	Wan\ shi\ da/ ka
American Express	美国运通卡	Mei^ guo/ yun\ tong- ka^

---
1. Let's Learn to Speak Some Mandarin
2. The name of Chinese currency. Like *Dollar* in the U.S. or *Euro* in Europe.

Chapter Eight
Safely Hidden Away
The Peninsula Hotel—Later Sunday Afternoon

Ling Ting Tong and Elwood had arrived home within a few minutes by subway. "Home" for them for several days had been the sumptuous Peninsula Suite on the 13th floor of the Peninsula Hotel, just a few blocks north of Tiananmen Square and The Forbidden City. The huge suite, larger than four or five normal houses in the U.S., usually rented for more than 10,000 CNY—Yuan Renminbi—or about 1,650 dollars per night. But, before leaving last week for Moscow, Ling Ting Tong had arranged for a 90-day lease at 8,500 CNY, or about 1,400 U.S. dollars per night. But a part of that arrangement had given the hotel the option to cancel the lease with five days notice—in case they had the opportunity to host some really rich and important party in the suite.

Finding no notice when they returned to the suite via its own elevator from the lobby, Mr. Ling said to Elwood, "We're okay here for another five days, at least. And it's a good place to hide. Who would ever think to look for us in one of the most posh and expensive hotel rooms in Beijing?"

"It's nice, all right," Elwood said, "but it sure costs a lot of Yuans. Why does Ar-Chee want to spend so much for a place to live?"

Looking surprised, Mr. Ling answered, "Elwood, it was I, Ling Ting Tong, who arranged for this suite. Ar-Chee would be happy living in a tree. But we have been very successful, and I believe we deserve some extra perks—a bit of luxury. Don't you agree?"

The question stressed Elwood's limited brain power. "I guess it's better than a tree, Mr. Ling. But there's enough room in here for 20 Chinese families. I might get lost. It kind of worries me."

"Many things worry you, Elwood. Just trust me. If you get lost, I will find you. Meantime, please just enjoy a nice place to live. And hide. Besides, I have an important assignment for you. In a few minutes, I want you to go, incognito, to the local police office. Find out what you can about where Ar-Chee might be. He must be in the hands of the police, but we need to know for sure."

Elwood pondered before saying, "I can do that, but can I just go in a taxi? I don't know about any cognitos."

Before Mr. Ling could explain, the sound of a buzzer pierced the parlor where they stood talking. Elwood went quickly to a speaker on the wall beside the private elevator. There he pushed a button and said, "Who is it?"

A familiar voice said, "It is I, your friend today. And always."

Mr. Ling said, "Let him come up. Push that green button."

Elwood said into the speaker, "Come on up," as he pushed the green button.

Ling Ting Tong said, "Elwood, you take the elevator back down. See what you can find out about Ar-Chee. And then report back to me."

The elevator door opened and two figures passed—one coming in, and the other going out.

The Beijing Suite—Fourth Floor of the Peninsula Hotel Later that Afternoon

No Quil had dropped the four cats and the dancing pig off at the downtown Peninsula Hotel where Socks had arranged for them to stay while they visited Beijing. Under orders from POTUS and the U.S. Secretary of State, the only two government officials in Washington, D.C. who even knew of the existence of Cats In Action, Socks had once again booked a suite in a four-star hotel for them.

Safely Hidden Away

Dusty often found herself at odds with the luxury of fine hotel suites. Cincinnati had reminded her often that they traveled for POTUS and that he had insisted that they travel first class. Further, Buzzer had reminded her that every time they went on a mission, they put their lives on the line for their country. He told her she should not be worried about spending a few hundred extra dollars.

Their suite, in fact, cost 3,800 Yuan Renminbi a day, or about 621 U.S. dollars.

Buzzer said, "Let's just find this porcupine quickly so we can all go back home to our little ranch in the Hill Country of Texas and get some rest. For a change. After all, we've been on the road almost continuously since late spring, tracking down Fred-X, the catnapping owl in Mexico and Italy; Carlos the puma in Argentina, France and Germany; and Ar-Chee in Moscow. As far as I'm concerned, it's time for a little vacation."

With Dusty now satisfied, for the moment at least, Luigi spoke up. "Luisa and I have been comparing notes," he said. "And we have some concerns about No Quil's cousin."

"No Way," Luisa said, "seems to us to be on the shady side. Just look at how quickly he emptied Mao's Mausoleum for us, and how fast he hurried us through that last search. There's nothing about him that strikes us as being on our side."

"In fact," Luigi went on, "we think he's likely in cahoots with that porcupine. And he's probably on Ar-Chee's payroll."

Dusty's first inclination was to pooh-pooh the twins. "You have nothing concrete to cause you to come to that conclusion," she said. "He did cooperate with us without question. Why do you say he's not to be trusted?"

Cincinnati, ever thoughtful, scratched his chin. "Dusty, I don't think we should just right away decide the twins are being silly. I've learned that their opinions are almost always right. While I didn't sense any bad vibes from No Way, that doesn't mean that Luigi and Luisa aren't onto something."

Buzzer, always with the last word on any subject as their leader, said, "I would certainly trust Luigi and Luisa before I would trust a complete stranger. And No Way is a complete stranger."

He turned to the twins. "Can you point to something—anything—specific that causes you to raise questions about No Way's loyalty?"

Luisa said, "Not yet, big brother. But we both had the same bad vibes."

Luigi piped up, "No Way just seemed to be too ready to help. Too eager to follow our directions without even knowing for sure who we are. Or why we wanted to find this porcupine, Mr. Ling. It's as if he had a plan. A plan he might have rehearsed with Ling Ting Tong in advance."

Luisa added, "And he seemed to be going through the motions of that plan. A plan to throw us off the track. Let me ask you, Buzzer. Can you think of any reason that Ling Ting Tong would not show up at noon as Ar-Chee had asked?"

"We think he was in that building," Luigi added, "and No Way helped him escape by throwing us off the track."

Buzzer and Cincinnati spoke quietly among themselves. And then Buzzer said, "I'll go with the twins' instincts. This No Way may, in fact, be bad news."

Cincinnati added, "So let's all keep our antennae out, our ears and eyes open. If he's working for Ar-Chee, we'll bag him, too."

Luigi said, "Luisa and I have a plan to smoke him out. If No Way is working against us, we'll find out right away."

"And what exactly do you two have in mind?" Dusty said accusingly.

This time Luisa spoke up. "Nothing, Dusty, that you would approve of. You never trust us. You never believe in us. Just let us follow our plan. And then you'll see what the two of us exactly have in mind."

Before Dusty could react, Buzzer stepped in. "We will all trust the twins. If they find that No Way is working against us, he'll be the first we stuff into a gunnysack and deliver to the Chinese authorities."

The twins exchanged two-paws up.

Then Luigi said, "Since we're no longer suspected of being too imaginative, would it be okay for Luisa and me to have some chocolate cake and ice cream?"

* Safely Hidden Away *

Dusty, still smarting from Buzzer's decision about the twins, said, "After your supper. Later this evening."

"Where will we be eating?" Luisa said.

"Downstairs in the Huang Ting Restaurant. They have Cantonese and seasonal Beijing specialties. I'm sure we'll all find something to enjoy," Buzzer said.

Luigi persisted, "Do they have chocolate cake and ice cream, though?"

"Yes!" Dusty shouted. "They have chocolate cake and ice cream. Now, leave it alone."

Sensing it was time to change the subject, Buzzer said, "We have some planning to do here. So let's all sit around that table and decide how we're going to go after this Ling Ting Tong."

Back on the 13th Floor in the Peninsula Suite

As Elwood stepped onto the elevator on his mission to find Ar-Chee's whereabouts, No Way stepped off, smiling. He said, "That plan of ours was pretty slick, no? I told you that hiding under Mao would work. Especially with me hurrying those porcupine chasers around the building, always being sure they never looked where you were hiding."

Mr. Ling said, "Yes, my friend and fellow agent, this time we fooled them. But they are smart. And they are clever. Most important, they won't give up until they have me—and you—in a cage inside the police offices."

No Way looked shocked. "Why me?" he said. "They don't want me. They're not looking for me."

"Because, my furry cat friend," No Quil said, "I will not be caught and turned in without taking you with me. Elwood can go free. He's not bright enough to cause the authorities any future problems. But you have helped me. And that makes you guilty. If I pay, you pay with me."

No Way looked shaken. "I want out. Right now. I'll return Ar-Chee's money, and you forget you ever heard of me. Is that a deal, Mr. Ling?"

Ling Ting Tong laughed. "No way, No Way!"

Do you think No Way will be able to escape being caught with Ling Ting Tong? What about Elwood? Will he find out what's happened to Ar-Chee? That he was captured last week in Moscow and is now in jail in Beijing? Since both the porcupine and porcupine chasers are, by odd coincidence, staying in the same hotel, do you think they might run into each other in the lobby? Or in one of the hotel's restaurants? And why do you think nobody in Washington, D.C. except POTUS and the Secretary of State even know about Cats In Action? What would happen if a goofy Congressman or two found out about the secret cats and the dancing pig? Would their secrecy be lost forever? Would their careers as catchers of bad guys come to an end?

✶ Safely Hidden Away ✶

让我们来学习一些普通话[1]

By Luigi and Luisa

Right now we have some work to do to plan how we're going to trap Ling Ting Tong. And figure out for sure if No Way is really working with him. But this evening, we'll be eating in one of the finest restaurants in Beijing—the Huang Ting in the Peninsula Hotel. Here are some words you will need to know about eating when you come to China.

English	Mandarin	Say it Like This
Table	桌子	Zhuo- zi
Chair	椅子	Yi^ zi
Tablecloth	台布	Tai/ bu\
Napkin	餐巾	Can- jin-
Plate	碟子	Die/ zi
Glass	玻璃杯	Bo- li bei-
Cup	茶杯	Cha/bei-
Saucer	茶杯碟	Cha/ bei- die/
Fork	叉子	Cha-zi
Knife	刀子	Dao- zi
Spoon	汤匙	Tang- chi/
Bowl	碗	Wan^
Chopsticks	筷子	Kuai\zi
Wait person	侍应	Shi\ying\
Menu	菜谱	Cai\ pu^

---

1. Let's Learn to Speak Some Mandarin

Chapter Nine
Laying Low ... Hunting High and Low

Peninsula Hotel—13th Floor—Peninsula Suite
Late Sunday Evening

No Way continued to argue for his release from the deal he had made with Ar-Chee and Ling Ting Tong to help them whenever they returned to Beijing. "I didn't intend to get into these crooked activities," He whined. "You didn't tell me I could end up in jail."

Ling Ting Tong had lost his patience with the complaining cat. "We're laying low, No Way. When Elwood gets back with the information about Ar-Chee, we're not leaving this hotel. In fact, we won't be leaving this suite for at least five days. And if you want to stay out of jail, you won't be leaving either."

No Way became even more distressed. "But I have to go to work at 7 a.m. in the morning. I'm the curator, the cat in charge of Mao Zedong's Mausoleum from 7:00 a.m. to 4:00 p.m. five days a week. My days off aren't until next Friday and Saturday. I can't stay here cooped up in this hotel with you and that stupid sloth. Officials will be looking for me. I will lose my job. And I might even be sent to re-training."

"Figure out what's worse—jail or re-training," Mr. Ling said. "Then you decide. The decision to stay or go doesn't matter to me. But you may be sure you will go to jail if I do. Just after I shoot about a dozen quills into your behind, that is."

No Way felt trapped. He felt doomed no matter which he decided to do—hide out in the hotel and risk losing his job and being sent to re-training ... or leaving the hotel and facing the chance of going to jail. He couldn't figure out how to escape either fate. Right now, he saw no way out.

Just then, the elevator signal sounded. Mr. Ling said, "Who's there?"

"It's me, Elwood. And I have the answer you sent me to find."

"Come on up," Ling Ting Tong said as he pushed the green button to activate the private elevator.

As the elevator opened and Elwood came into the parlor, No Way made his choice. He raced for the open elevator door, jumped in and quickly pressed the DOWN button. *If I have to run away . . . completely vanish from my job and Beijing,* he thought, *I will not go to jail or re-training. I'll lose myself in the countryside and live the life of a beggar. No Jail. No retraining. But . . . I will not return Ar-Chee's money. I can live on it for quite a while.*

"Let him go!" Mr. Ling said as Elwood instinctively tried to grab No Way to keep him from getting into the elevator. "He has just signed his fate. Elwood, we won't work with traitors, will we?"

"Is No Way a traitor, Mr. Ling?" Elwood said, once again confused.

"Yes, Elwood. He's just run out on us. So we can't depend on his help in the future." Seeing Elwood looking terrified, Mr. Ling added, "But that's okay. We'll hide out in this hotel until those pesky cats and their pig friend decide to give up and go home. They will never find us here."

He took a chair beside a big window overlooking downtown Beijing and said, "Now, tell me what you've learned of our friend Ar-Chee?"

Peninsula Hotel—4th Floor—Beijing Suite
At the Same Time

Because of their late lunch, the four cats of the CIA and Cincinnati the dancing pig had decided to put off having dinner until late in the evening. As they left the Huang Ting Restaurant and headed for the elevator to their fourth floor suite, Luigi and Luisa both saw No Way scuttling out of an elevator and racing across the hotel's lobby. "He's running like his tail's on fire," Luigi said. "Don't you wonder what he was doing here in this hotel?"

Luisa, ever vigilant, noted that No Way had come from what

seemed to be a private elevator. "We'll need to find out where that elevator goes," she said. "Wherever it stops, that's where No Way was visiting."

As they got into their elevator, Buzzer reminded them, "Remember, we decided that our first act in chasing down Ling Ting Tong would be to question No Way. Luisa and Luigi have a plan to uncover who he's really working for. So, first thing in the morning, the twins will go to Tiananmen Square—to No Way's office in Mao Zedong's Mausoleum..."

Luigi interrupted, "And we'll get the truth out of that little weasel. Right, Luisa?"

"Right, Luigi!" she said.

Dusty spoke up. "You're not going alone. I won't hear of it."

Buzzer said quickly, "Of course not. The three of us will be with them. We'll just keep out of sight."

As they went into their suite, Dusty Louise said, "I don't know about the rest of you, but I'm very, very tired. I suggest we all get some sleep. We'll all be better able to think clearly in the morning."

With that, she went into the bedroom she would sleep in alone. Buzzer and Cincinnati said, "Good night," and went into the bedroom with twin beds where they would sleep. While the group had been at dinner, the concierge had arranged to have a roll-away bed with two pillows set up in the parlor—the same kind of bed the twins had become accustomed to sharing in all their adventures.

Luisa, looking mischievous and not at all tired, said, "How long do we wait, Luigi?"

"Let's give them 15 or 20 minutes, Luisa. Then we make the phone call."

At the Same Time Back Upstairs in the Peninsula Suite

As he sipped at a snifter of brandy and puffed on a large Cuban cigar, Ling Ting Tong said, "Tell me what you found out, Elwood. Do you know where Ar-Chee is right now?"

Elwood scratched his head and pondered, "First off," he said, "I went in a taxi. What's a cognito, Mr. Ling? I was afraid to ask for one. Never been in one. It might be too scary."

* Laying Low . . . Hunting High and Low *

"Never mind about the cognito, Elwood. And I'm glad you took a taxi. So where did you go?"

"Like you said, Mr. Ling, I went to the police office. I told that taxi driver to take me to the nearest one. And he did. We got there real quick. He wanted to be paid and to get away fast. He said he didn't like hanging around any police offices."

This is going to take awhile, Ling Ting Tong thought, *but I have to be patient.* "Okay, Elwood, so you're at the police station. What happened there?"

"Well," Elwood began, "I went inside. And there was this officer sitting behind a big, high desk. So I asked him, 'Where is Ar-Chee?' And he said, 'Who is Ar-Chee?' So I said, 'Ar-Chee's a big panda bear, and he's been missing. We thought he might be in jail.'"

"What did he say, Elwood?" Mr. Ling asked.

"He said he didn't know anything about any panda, but he would check. And he did. And, sure enough, he made a few phone calls and then he told me that a big panda named Ar-Chee had been arrested in Moscow. And I could find him at the Qincheng Prison."

"Good work, Elwood. Now we know what happened to Ar-Chee for sure. I guess that's when you came back here, right?"

"Oh, no, Mr. Ling. I wanted to do a good job. So I thought I should go to see for myself that Ar-Chee was really there."

"You did what?" Ling Ting Tong said, wondering what might be coming next.

"This time I asked about a cognito to take me there, but nobody knew what I was talking about. So I took another taxi. The prison's out north of town, you know."

"You actually went to Qincheng Prison? Was Ar-Chee there?"

"Oh, yes, sir. He was there, all right. We had us a nice visit. I told him about the porcupine chasers coming after you. And he said to tell you to get your quills up and shoot them in the behind."

Ling Ting Tong asked, "Did you have to sign any papers before you visited with Ar-Chee?"

Elwood smiled a proud smile. "I sure did. Signed my name

pretty as you please."

"Did you give them an address where you lived?"

"Yes, sir, I did. Told them right on top of the Peninsula Hotel in a big suite. But they didn't believe me. They laughed really hard. And they told me to forget it and go on in. So I did."

Back Downstairs in the Beijing Suite—15 Minutes Later

It was dark in the parlor as the twins sat on the edge of their bed waiting for Dusty, Buzzer and Cincinnati to go to sleep. Luigi tiptoed quietly on little kitten feet to Dusty's door and then on to Buzzer and Cincinnati's door, and came back to Luisa. "They're all snoring, Luisa, so I guess it's time. You? Or me?"

"I'll do it this time," Luisa said. She picked up the telephone and dialed four numbers. Then she said quietly in Mandarin, "Room Service? This is Dusty Louise Giaccomazza in the Beijing Suite on the fourth floor. Would you please send up two bowls of vanilla ice cream and two pieces of chocolate cake right away? And, Room Service, add 50 Yuan to the bill for the bellman, and have him knock softly twice and just leave the cake and ice cream on a tray outside the door. You got that? Thank you."

She put down the phone, gave Luigi a high two, and walked quietly to wait by the door to the hallway.

Do you think No Way will be at his job in Tiananmen Square in the morning when Luigi and Luisa go to question him? What do you think they will find out? And what about Elwood's visit to Qincheng Prison and Ar-Chee? He said the guards didn't believe he lives in a posh suite in a big hotel, but maybe he gave away a little too much information? Will that slip-up by Elwood cause Ling Ting Tong to change his mind about hiding in the hotel for five days? And what about the twins? Do you think Dusty will find out about them ordering more chocolate cake and ice cream from Room Service? If she does, do you think she will put them in time out?

* Beijing Ding-a-Ling: Mao of the CIA *

让我们来学习一些普通话[1]

By Luisa and Luigi

By now you know that we spend a lot of time in hotels in foreign countries. If you should visit China and stay in a hotel, there will be many words you will need to know. Here are a few to help you.

English	Mandarin	Say it Like This
Hotel	酒店	Jiu^ dian\
Room	房间	Fang-- jian-
Suite	套房	Tao\ fang/
Check in	入住登记	Ru\ zhu\ deng- ji\
Check out	退房登记	Tui\ fang/ deng- ji\
Bellman	行李员	Xing/ li^ yuan/
Concierge	礼宾部	Li^ bing- bu\
Coffee shop	咖啡店	Ka- fei- dian\
Elevator	电梯	Dian\ ti-
Restaurant	餐厅	Can- ting-
Desk clerk	总台	Zong^ tai/
Luggage	行李	Xing/ li^
Room key	房匙	Fang/ shi\
Bed	床	Chuang/
Sheet	床单	Chuang/ dan-
Pillow	枕头	Zhrn^ tou/
Bathroom	浴室	Yu\ shi\
Towel	毛巾	Mao/ jin-
Room Service	客房服务	Ke\ fang/ fu/ wu\

---

1. Let's Learn to Speak Some Mandarin

Chapter Ten
Truth... or Jail
Peninsula Suite—Peninsula Hotel—Early Monday Morning

Ling Ting Tong had slept little Sunday night. The business of Elwood's visit to the prison had kept him tossing and turning. He thought, *Did the guards really not believe Elwood lived at the Peninsula Hotel? Whether they believed it or not, it's still a matter of written record. I have to get that off the record. Those cats will find it out sooner or later.*

He made coffee and heated up some buttered rolls. Then he woke Elwood up. "Have some breakfast, Elwood. Then I have another important assignment for you."

"What can I do for you today?" Elwood asked, sipping coffee and munching of a roll. "If it's real important, maybe you should come with me."

"I know you can handle this by yourself," Mr. Ling said. "It's a repair job."

"What am I going to fix? I'm not a real good fixer, you know."

"You're going to go back to the prison and give the guards a new address." Ling Ting Tong carefully wrote out an address on a piece of paper. "Here, this is where you live now. Give it to the guards and tell them you were just confused yesterday. Tell them you want to set the record straight."

Elwood took the paper, looked at it and said, "Where is this address? I don't live there."

"Of course you don't, Elwood. But we don't want the authorities thinking you live here, do we? They might just track us down, and then you might have to go to jail. Remember?"

"Yes," Elwood said. "I remember, but shouldn't I know where this address is? What if they ask and I have to say I don't know where I live today. If I didn't know yesterday, and I don't know today, they might get suspicious, don't you think?"

Of course, Ling Ting Tong thought. *What's wrong with me? Even Elwood is thinking more clearly than me. I've got to get my mind cleared out.*

"You're right, Elwood. Of course you need to know where the address is in the city. Here, look at this map." He pointed to a street between downtown and Capital International Airport. "The address is right here. Why don't you have the taxi take you by this address. It's not far out of the way if you're going to the prison, anyway. Then you'll know not only where the apartment building is located, but also exactly what it looks like—just in case anybody should ask."

Finishing his breakfast, Elwood said, "Can you give me some money? I might not have enough Yuans to go to all these places."

Mr. Ling handed him 500 Yuans. "Now, go see that the address from yesterday is changed on the record. Then come straight back here. I'll be waiting for you. We'll have an extra special lunch."

Elwood tucked the Yuans into a pocket, waved to Mr. Ling, and stepped into the private elevator. "See you soon," he said as the doors closed.

Mao's Mausoleum—Tiananmen Square—Monday Morning

After their breakfast, Luigi and Luisa had spent some time sharpening their plan to get to the truth about No Way. Now, as they approached Mao Zedong's Mausoleum, they were ready to turn on the charm. And the heat.

While Buzzer, Cincinnati and Dusty wandered around inside the building, the twins skipped up the stairs to No Way's office. The door was open, so they stepped in to be greeted by a woman who apparently worked for No Way. The woman said, "Mr. No is not receiving guests today. You must go back downstairs. Call for an appointment if you wish to speak to him tomorrow."

Luisa batted her eyelashes and put on her cute look. "I think Mr. No will see us. Please tell him Luigi and Luisa are here. He met us yesterday."

"He really helped us, too," Luigi said. "We've come to thank him. It's very important that we see him."

* Truth . . . or Jail *

The woman smiled and slipped into No Way's inner office. "There are two really cute kittens here to see you Sir. I know you said no visitors, but they say they've come to thank you for something you helped them with yesterday. Will you see them?"

"Ah," No Way said. "That must be Luigi and Luisa. Are there two larger cats and a dancing pig with them?"

"No, just the two kittens. And they are Luigi and Luisa. At least those are the names they gave me."

No Way sat back in his chair. "As long as they're alone, go ahead and send them in. And would you bring in some tea, please. We must be gracious to our guests. Even little kittens."

"Come in, come in," No Way said as the twins stepped into the room. "It's good to see you again so soon. How can I help you today?"

Luigi spoke up, "Oh, Mr. No, there are many ways you can help us. Let's start with the truth."

No Way was taken aback. "The truth? About what, pray tell?"

Luisa said, "About yesterday. And about the porcupine we were looking for. Where did you hide him?"

No Way began to fidget. "I'm sure I don't know what you're talking about. I know nothing about any hidden porcupine."

"Well, first, we wanted to thank you for helping us yesterday," Luigi said. "But now that we've done that, shall we begin at the beginning?"

"If you say so," No Way said, hesitating. "What's on your minds?"

"Tell us about Ar-Chee." Luisa said. "How long have you been working for him?"

No Way tried not to look guilty, but lies were written all over his face. "Ar-Chee?" he said. "Who is this panda?"

"Ah, ha!" Luigi said. "If you don't know him, how did you know he's a panda?"

"It's time to come clean, Mr. No," Luisa said, adding, "We're going to sit right here until you tell us how much Ar-Chee paid you to hide Ling Ting Tong. And don't tell us you don't know that portly porcupine. We know you helped hide him. He was here yesterday. And you know it. No more baloney, No Way."

* 69 *

* Beijing Ding-a-Ling: Mao of the CIA *

"One more thing," Luigi said. "We saw you leaving a private elevator in the Peninsula Hotel last night. You seemed to be in a big hurry. Who were you visiting at that hour?"

By now, No Way had begun to tremble. He looked wild-eyed around the room. Suddenly he made a run for the door, slamming it behind him and locking the twins in his office.

Luigi began to count: "One, two, three, four, five, six, seven, eight . . . now! Just about now No Way has run right into the waiting arms of Buzzer, Cincinnati and Dusty Louise."

"Once again, we were right. He knows a lot of stuff that can help us capture Ling Ting Tong," Luisa said. And then she began to count: "One, two, three, four, five, six . . . now!"

Just as she'd said "now," the office door opened. In walked Buzzer, Dusty and Cincinnati, who carried a small gunny sack with Mr. No inside, squirming and yelling.

The woman who had let the twins into No Way's office followed them in, demanding to know what was going on. "Why do you have No Way in that sack?" she said. "What are you going to do with him?"

Luigi answered, "What we do with him depends completely on whether he has decided to work with us."

Luisa added, "And not against us."

Cincinnati, setting No Way's sack on the top of his desk, turned to the woman. "Please sit down and join us, Ma'am," he said. "I think you'll find our conversation with Mr. No quite interesting. And revealing."

Buzzer and Dusty slowly removed the sack, leaving No Way sitting on top of his desk. Buzzer turned to the woman, "Please lock the door, Ma'am. We don't want Mr. No to try to run for it again."

Then he motioned to the twins. "Your turn again," Buzzer said.

No Way began to plead, "I don't want to go to jail."

Luigi and Luisa jumped up on the desk on either side of Mr. No. Luisa said, "Then answer our questions."

Luigi added, "Tell us what we want to know, No Way, and we'll cut you a deal."

* Truth ... or Jail *

"What kind of deal?" Mr. No asked. "Can you keep me out of jail?"

Luigi smiled. "There might just be a way, No Way."

To everyone's surprise, Dusty Louise added, "But if you don't tell us everything, there'll be no way, No Way."

Do you think Elwood will succeed in changing his address for the record? Or will he somehow give away Ling Ting Tong's real address? And what about No Way? Will he come clean and tell the CIA cats and Cincinnati the dancing pig what they want to know? Will he help them capture Ling Ting Tong in return for not having to go to jail? Or was Luigi fibbing when he said No Way might not go to jail if he cooperated? And what do you think caused Dusty, who is usually quiet, to speak up—almost threateningly—to No Way?

✱ Beijing Ding-a-Ling: Mao of the CIA ✱

让我们来学习一些普通话[1]

By Luigi and Luisa

Questioning No Way is hard work. When we finish getting him to come clean and tell us everything he knows about Ling Ting Tong, we're going to be hungry. And you already know our favorite food is ice cream. So you will know what to order in China, here are some ice cream flavors to learn.

English	Mandarin	Say it Like This
Ice cream	冰淇淋	Bing- qi/ lin/
Chocolate	巧克力	Qiao^ ke- li\
Strawberry	草莓	Cao^mei/
Peach	桃子	Tao/ zi
Raspberry	覆盘子	Fu\ pen/ zi
Neapolitan	三色雪糕	San- se \ xue^ gao-
Chocolate chip	巧克力片	Qiao^ ke- li\pian\
Cookie dough	饼干面团	Bing^ gan- mian\ tuan/
Pistachio	开心果	Kai- xin- guo^
Banana nut	香蕉果仁味	Xiang-jiao- guo^ren/ wei\
Vanilla	香草	Xiang- cao^

---

1. Let's Learn to Speak Some Mandarin

Chapter Eleven
Who's Going to the Hoosegow?
Mao's Mausoleum—Monday Morning

Cincinnati and the cats of the CIA had decided to question No Way right in his own office. Luigi, without any approval from any authorities, had promised No Way he wouldn't have to go to jail if he told them the complete truth. And decided to actually help them capture Ling Ting Tong, the multi-lingual and portly porcupine. Remember that Mr. Ling remained the brains behind Ar-Chee's opium-smuggling operation. A business that had made both the panda and the porcupine very, very rich.

Nobody seemed to notice when the woman who worked for No Way slipped quietly from the room.

Buzzer Louis pulled Luigi aside for a private talk. "Why did you promise Mr. No that he could avoid jail—go free—if he spills the beans, Luigi? Are you sure we can make that guarantee?"

"Well, big brother," Luigi said. "If he helps us by telling us everything he knows so we can capture Ling Ting Tong, then who besides us knows that he has been paid by Ar-Chee? And that he hid the porcupine yesterday—hid him from us?"

Buzzer said, "I suppose nobody but the porcupine really knows. Don't you think Ling Ting Tong will try to take Mr. No to prison with him?"

"Sure he will, Buzzy," Luigi said, "but it will be his word against ours. Don't you think the Chinese authorities will believe us before they will believe a crooked, quill-shooting porcupine?"

Buzzer frowned. "So you expect us to lie to save No Way from prison? That's not the way we do things, Luigi. And you know it."

"We don't have to lie at all," Luigi said. "We just don't have to tell everything we know, do we? We will just say that No Way was a big help to us in our mission to capture Ling Ting Tong."

Buzzer thought about that. Then he said, "Still, No Way has been paid by Ar-Chee to hide Ling Ting Tong. And to throw us off the track. You don't think he should be able to keep that money, do you?"

"There's no way No Way's going to keep whatever Ar-Chee paid him," Luigi said. "Leave that to Luisa and me. We'll get every Yuan back."

"And what should we do with that money, Luigi? It might be a lot," Buzzer said.

"Luisa has already figured that out, Buzzer," Luigi said. "She's made contact with a group of orphanages in Hefei, down south of here. We'll send all the money to them. You know orphanages can always use extra money. Right?"

"Okay, then," Buzzer said. "As usual, you two have figured everything out ahead of Cincinnati, Dusty and me. So go ahead and start getting some answers from this creep. I don't like turning him loose, but if we have to, then we have to."

Meanwhile
Back at the Peninsula Hotel in Ling Ting Tong's Suite

Elwood had been gone for about an hour on the mission to see the apartment where he was supposed to pretend to live. And to correct his address in the records of visitors to Ar-Chee at Qincheng prison. The private elevator buzzer sounded. Mr. Ling hoped the visitor would not be Elwood. *He hasn't been gone long enough to finish the job I sent him to do*, he thought.

Since the porcupine didn't know who might be trying to use the elevator, he pushed the speaker button and, disguising his voice, said, "This is the maid. Nobody's here right now."

A woman's voice replied, "Ling Ting Tong, you idiot, you're in trouble. Big trouble. The cats and the pig have captured No Way, and I think he's going to sing like a canary."

Mr. Ling pushed the green button. "Come up. And hurry!"

The woman said, "I can only go as fast as the elevator will take me. What's wrong with you? Have you gone cracker-porcupine? Sit down. I bring shocking news."

"Just get up here!" Ling Ting Tong said.

Back in No Way's Office

As the twins had planned, Luisa began the questioning. She would be nice. Pretend to be understanding. To be a true friend of No Way. If Mr. No hesitated, Luigi would jump in as the bad guy. "Think of me as *The Hammer*," he had told Luisa.

"So, Mr. No," Luisa began, "How long have you known Ar-Chee and Ling Ting Tong?"

Frightened, No Way glanced around the room. Every face stared at him sternly, except Luisa's. She was smiling.

No Way offered an answer. "I first met Ar-Chee several years ago. He introduced me to Ling Ting Tong just recently. They said they were going to Russia to arrange some business in Moscow."

Luisa continued, "Did they tell you what kind of business?"

"No, just that they hoped to arrange some kind of local distribution arrangement," No Way answered.

"And you didn't know what they wanted distributed in Moscow?" Luisa asked. "Before you answer, remember, please, that our offer to keep you from prison depends on total cooperation from you. One little fib, and BANG! You're in the hoosegow."

"Hoosegow? What is a hoosegow?" Mr. No asked, looking even more scared.

Luigi spoke up, "You don't want to know, No Way. It's worse than any prison you could ever imagine. So you just answer Luisa's questions."

"Okay," No Way said. "They told me they were smuggling drugs. But I didn't know what kind of drugs. And I still don't."

Again, Luigi spoke up, "So you knew you would be helping them do something not only illegal, but also just plain horrible? Isn't that right?"

No Way was shaking now. Cincinnati turned to Buzzer and said softly, "Luigi and Luisa have broken him. He'll tell us everything he knows. We just have to be sure he doesn't start making things up to try to make himself look less bad in our eyes."

Seeming to have read Cincinnati's mind, Luigi spoke sharply, "I warn you, No Way, not to be making up anything you don't absolutely know to be a fact. There's no way we're going to be-

Beijing Ding-a-Ling: Mao of the CIA

lieve any lies. Are we clear on that, Sir?"

No Way nodded. "I don't know much, but I will tell you everything. Just no hoosegow, please."

Luisa began again. "Did you ever work for Ar-Chee before yesterday?"

"No. I swear that was the first time," No Way said, his voice quaking and tears rolling slowly down his cheeks from both eyes.

Luigi decided now was the time to go for the goal. "How much did Ar-Chee pay you to hide Ling Ting Tong?"

"He paid me 100,000 Yuan Renminbi," No Way said. "I will give it all back."

"Yes, you will give it all back," Luisa said. "Hand it over."

"That's a lot of money, No Way," Luigi said. Turning to Dusty Louise, he added. "It's 16,300 dollars in U.S. currency."

Luisa piped up, "Actually, it's $16,345.02—if you want to be exact." She grinned at Luigi, who thought that correction to somehow be funny.

He snickered.

And then he turned serious.

No Way handed Luisa an envelope. "It's still sealed," he said. "I haven't even opened it."

Luigi said, "Don't you think it might have been a good idea to count the money given to you by a big-time international gangster? Are you really that trusting?"

Luisa said but one word. "Naïve."

Luigi pulled himself to his full height, saluted Buzzer, Dusty and Cincinnati, and then said, "That's enough small talk. No Way, where can we find Ling Ting Tong? Remember, one lie and it's the hoosegow for you."

No Way gave them all a pleading look. "I swear, he's staying in the Peninsula Suite on the 13th floor of the Peninsula Hotel, He said nobody would ever guess he would hide out in such a posh place. He's there right now."

Buzzer said to Cincinnati, "Get in touch with No Quil. Ask him to meet us in the lobby of the Peninsula Hotel right away." Then he turned to No Way."We're going to take you with us."

"Please, please, no." No Way said. "If Ling Ting Tong sees

me with you, then he'll know I've turned him in. And he'll shoot dozens of quills into me. Please, let me stay here. Lock me in. I won't go anywhere. I promise."

Dusty looked around the room. "Where is that woman who was here when we arrived?"

Where is that woman, anyway? Do you think she's the one who went to warn Ling Ting Tong? If so, is she also on Ar-Chee the panda's payroll? Will Cincinnati and the cats of the CIA trust No Way to stay in his office while they go to the hotel to try to capture Ling Ting Tong? Would you trust him to stay there? And when they get to the hotel, do you think Elwood will have returned from his mission? Will Ling Ting Tong still be hiding in the Peninsula Suite on the 13th floor of the Peninsula Hotel? Will the woman from No Way's office still be there, too?

* Beijing Ding-a-Ling: Mao of the CIA *

让我们来学习一些普通话[1]

By Luisa and Luigi

Right now, it's Monday morning while we're hot on the trail of Ling Ting Tong. We also know the month is August. But what if you came to China at another time of year? How would you know what to call the days of the week and the months of the year? Here are some words to help you keep up with time in Mandarin.

English	Mandarin	Say it Like This
Day	日子	Ri\zi
Monday	星期一	Xing-qi-yi
Tuesday	星期二	Xing-qi-er\
Wednesday	星期三	Xing-qi-san-
Thursday	星期四	Xing-qi-si\
Friday	星期五	Xing-qi-wu^
Saturday	星期六	Xing-qi liu\
Sunday	星期天	Xing-qi- tian-
Week	星期	Xing- qi
Month	月	Yue\
January	一月	Yi- yue\
February	二月	Er\ yue\
March	三月	San - yue\
April	四月	Si\ yue\
May	五月	Wu^ yue\
June	六月	Liu\ yue-\
July	七月	Qi- yue\
August	八月	BT - yue \

---

1. Let's Learn to Speak Some Mandarin

* Who's Going to the Hoosegow! *

English	Mandarin	Say it Like This
September	九月	Jiu^yue\
October	十月	Shi/ yue\
November	十一月	Shi/ yue\
December	十二月	Shi/ er\ yue\
Season	季节	Ji\ jie/
Winter	冬天	Dong-tian-
Spring	春天	Chun- tian-
Summer	夏天	Xia\ tian-
Fall	秋天	Qiu-tian-

Part Three
If at First You Don't Succeed

Chapter Twelve
Porcupine on the Lam
Lobby of the Peninsula Hotel

Buzzer and Cincinnati had decided not to leave No Way in his office, locked or otherwise. Instead, they had brought him to the Peninsula Hotel and tied him up in their rooms—the Beijing Suite on the 4th floor.

While Buzzer and Cincinnati were securing No Way, Dusty Louise and the twins had found the hotel security office. Flashing their credentials, they convinced the hotel's chief of security to disable the private elevator that went only to Ling Ting Tong's hideaway on the 13th floor. With No Way now under control, Buzzer and Cincinnati met Luigi, Luisa, Dusty and the security chief in the lobby.

"Can we get to the 13th floor any way besides the private elevator?" Buzzer asked.

The security chief answered, "You can take the regular elevators to the 12th floor and then go up the fire emergency staircase to the 13th. But you will need this key to open the door to the Peninsula Suite."

With that, he handed Cincinnati a key and pointed to an elevator that would take them to the 12th floor.

Just then, No Quil arrived. Buzzer said to him, "We think Mr. Ling is in the suite on the 13th floor. The private elevator to that suite has been shut off. And we're going up there by way of the fire stairs from the 12th floor. We need you to stand guard right here to be sure Ling Ting Tong doesn't try to escape by running down the stairs. Or taking a regular elevator. Call us on my satellite phone if you see him."

Cincinnati added, "Don't let him get out of your sight. We'll be right behind you if he shows up down here."

Quickly the group rode to the 12th floor and ran up the stairs to the Peninsula Suite. Carefully, so as not to make much noise, Cincinnati turned the key on the fire door, and they crept down the hallway to Ling Ting Tong's rooms.

Cincinnati whispered, "Everybody stand back." With that, he backed up, ran at the door and crashed through it right into the porcupine's parlor, apparently forgetting that they had been given a key to open it. Quickly they searched all the rooms, closets, pantries and cupboards.

Nobody was there, but the beginnings of what looked to be a sumptuous lunch were laid out on the kitchen counter.

"He left in a hurry," Luigi said. "This lunch is half ready." He quickly scanned the counters to be sure there was no chocolate cake. Seeing none, he added, "Somebody tipped him off. And he's made a run for it."

Buzzer's phone rang. He answered it and listened for a few moments. As he disconnected the call, he said, "Well, we know now who tipped him off. That woman who was in No Way's office earlier? No Quil just caught her trying to sneak out of the hotel. She had first tried to get No Way to go from our Suite with her. But it seems he refused. He's still in our rooms on the 4th floor. That's where we're going now to meet No Quil and the mysterious woman."

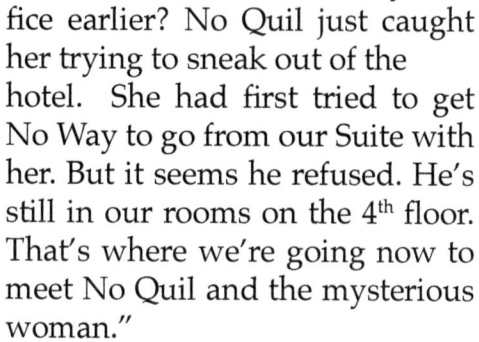

The hotel's security chief agreed to station one of his helpers in Ling Ting Tong's suite—just in case the porcupine might try to return. "It looks like he's left everything here. Maybe he'll try to sneak back in to get something important he left behind."

As they started for the broken

door, suddenly a sloth, panting and perspiring, stepped into the parlor. "Holy mackerel," the sloth said, "what happened to that door? And why doesn't the elevator work? And who are all of you? And where is Ling Ting Tong?"

Luigi and Luisa stepped forward. Luisa said, "We're asking the questions here. So who are you? And what are you doing here?"

The sloth seemed once again confused. He tried to answer, worried that Luisa and Luigi might try to take him to prison. "My name is Elwood," he said.

Then he stopped answering.

Luigi said, "She asked you what you're doing here?"

Elwood, ever more confused, said, "I think I live here. Or maybe I live in an apartment on the way to Qincheng Prison. That's where I've been. Honest, I just got back, and I had to climb up 13 floors of stairs because Mr. Ling didn't answer the elevator buzzer. And the elevator doesn't work, anyway."

Buzzer stepped in. "Slow down, Elwood. Do you work for Mr. Ling?"

"I did. I mean I do. I think. He sent me on a mission to see the apartment where I don't really live but pretend to. Live there, that is. Then I went to Qincheng Prison to fix my address from yesterday, just like Mr. Ling said. I changed the address from yesterday to that apartment where I don't really live."

He paused, looking forlorn. "Can I live here, now? Still, I mean?"

Cincinnati whispered to Buzzer, "This Elwood's clearly a few bricks shy of a load, Buzz. Getting answers from him may take a long discussion. Let's take him with us down to the 4th floor. We can put him in a bedroom and let the twins get him to fess up while you and Dusty and No Quil and I find out what the story is with this mysterious woman."

Buzzer motioned to Elwood. "Come with us, Elwood. We'll talk some more."

Elwood shrank back, obviously afraid. Luisa spoke up, "It's okay, Elwood. We're not going to hurt you. We just want to talk."

Elwood moved ahead. Hesitating, he said, "Is Mr. Ling in

trouble? Did you take him to prison?"

Luigi said, "No, Elwood. Right now, Mr. Ling seems to be missing. We need to find him, but we don't know exactly where to look."

Elwood's face lit up. He said, with enthusiasm, "Oh. I'll bet I know where he is. I can help you find him."

Luigi looked at Luisa. They grinned at one another, and Luisa said, "Good, Elwood. You can help us play hide and seek with him."

The Beijing Suite—4th Floor

The hotel's security chief had gone ahead of the group to take No Way to the security offices for safe keeping. No Way had told him, "I don't want to run away. I'm here to help find Ling Ting Tong. He's a double-crosser and a crook, you know."

The security chief had given No Way a cup of tea and suggested it would be better if he didn't say any more "until those cats and that pig come back to get you."

So No Way sat silently, leafing through a magazine called *Mao-Mao: Cats of China*.

While Luigi and Luisa, winking at Buzzer, took Elwood into a bedroom to explain him how they would all play hide and seek with Ling Ting Tong, Buzzer, Dusty, Cincinnati and No Quil began to question the mysterious woman.

Dusty spoke first. "You were with us an hour ago in No Way's office. Do you work there?"

The woman, tall and dressed in a black pants suit, gave Dusty a surly look. "Yes," she said. "I am Mr. No's assistant. And he's a very important person in Beijing. I suggest you release him at once."

Dusty smiled. "Unfortunately, you, Madam, are not in charge here. We will tend to Mr. No appropriately." She paused, and then added, "Do you have a name?"

The woman bristled. "Everybody has a name."

"Would you care to tell us what it is?" Dusty said. "Or shall we just ask No way?"

Sticking out her chin, the woman said, "He won't tell you."

Dusty laughed. "*Au contraire*. He's downstairs right now, tell-

* Beijing Ding-a-Ling: Mao of the CIA *

ing hotel security everything."

Buzzer stepped in. "We know you tipped off Ling Ting Tong that we were coming for him. How much did he pay you for that service?"

The woman lost her temper. "That cheapskate! Not only did he not pay me, he didn't even bother to thank me. He's an evil porcupine."

Cincinnati grinned, and then said, "I'm sorry for you. But it's a little bit late for you to be finding out who and what Mr. Ling really is. Just know, for right now, that he has gotten you in a lot of trouble. A whole lot of trouble."

Where do you think Ling Ting Tong has gone? Do you think Elwood really knows where to find him? Will Elwood fall for Luigi and Luisa's trick of pretending to play hide and seek? And what about the mysterious woman? Who is she? And what will the Cats of the CIA and Cincinnati do with her? Turn her over to No Quil? But she's not a porcupine, so what would he do with her?

* Porcupine on the Lam *

让我们来学习一些普通话[1]

By Luigi and Luisa

Now you know about the days, weeks, months and seasons. But what about the time during each day? If you have appointments in China, you'll need to know how to tell time. Here are some words to help you stay on schedule each day.

English	Mandarin	Say it Like This
Sunup	日出	Ri\ chu-
Sundown	日落	Ri\ luo\
Noon	中午	Zhong- wu^
Midnight	凌晨	Ling/ cheng/
Morning	早上	Zao^ shang\
Afternoon	下午	Xia\ wu^
Evening	晚上	Wan^ shang\
Night	夜晚	Ye\ wan^
8 a.m.	早上8点	Zao^shang\ 8 dian^
10 a.m.	上午10点	Shang\ wu^ 10 dian^
2 p.m.	下午2点	Xia\ wu^ 2 dian^
4 p.m.	下午4点	Xia\ wu ^ 4 dian^
6 p.m.	下午6点	Xia\ wu^ 6 dsian^
8 p.m.	晚上8点	Wan^ shang\ 8 dian^
10 p.m.	晚上10点	Wan^ shang\ 10 dian^
Bed time	晚休时间	Wan^ xiu- shi/ jian-
2 a.m.	凌晨2点	Ling/ cheng/ 2 dian^
4 a.m.	凌晨4点	Ling/ cheng/ 4 dian^
6 a.m.	早上6点	Zao^ shang\ 6 dian^

---

1. Let's Learn to Speak Some Mandarin

Chapter Thirteen
A Sloth in Time
Beijing Suite—4th Floor—Peninsula Hotel

While Buzzer, Cincinnati and Dusty Louise questioned the mysterious woman who continued to refuse to tell them her name, the twins—Luigi and Luisa—took the sloth Elwood into one of the suite's bedrooms to question him. Except they had decided to explain a new kind of the game, hide and seek, to the not-so-bright sloth.

Elwood spoke first. "When can we start playing hide and seek? I really like that game."

Luisa answered, "We'll play soon, Elwood. But first we have to explain how to play this new kind of hide and seek."

"I already know how to play normal hide and seek," Elwood said. "What makes this game different?"

"That's what we're going to talk about right now," Luigi said. "Luisa will tell you all about it."

Elwood turned his attention to Luisa. "Tell me," he said.

Luisa began, "Well, you see, Elwood, in this game only one player gets to hide. All the rest of us try to find that player. And that player who's hiding can go anywhere to hide. He might just go somewhere in China, but he might go anywhere in the world for all we know."

Elwood interrupted. "Can I be the first person to hide when we start this game? I'm good at hiding. Ask Mr. Ling. He'll tell you I'm a good hider."

Luigi spoke up. "The game has already begun. And Mr. Ling is the first one to go hide. So he's left the hotel to hide somewhere where he thinks we won't be able to find him."

He paused to let the concept sink in to Elwood's somewhat

slow-moving brain. Then he continued, "So our job is to go out there into the world and find him. We'll work as a team, And, Elwood, you can be the leader of the team."

Elwood sat back, a frown crossing his face. "I'm not a good leader. I don't know how. But Mr. Ling and Mr. Ar-Chee both told me I'm a really good follower. Are you sure you want me to be the leader?"

Luisa said, "Remember, Elwood, that I said this is a different kind of hide and seek? In this game, the best follower gets to be the leader. And that's you."

"Besides," Luigi said, "you have special information that the rest of us don't have."

"I don't ever have any information until Mr. Ling tells me," Elwood said, still looking worried.

"Oh, but in this case you're the only one who has any information," Luisa said.

Luigi added, "And you have it all."

This potential responsibility to lead was making Elwood very nervous. His mental process continued to try to catch up with what the twins had told him. So he just sat in his chair, looking perplexed and gesturing with one paw and then another as he sorted out his confusion.

Suddenly he brightened. "Okay," he said. "I'm all caught up now. But there is one thing."

"What's that, Elwood?" Luisa asked, winking at Luigi.

The sloth grimaced, screwed his face up into total confusion, and said, "I don't know what it is that you say I know. What don't I know that I know?"

Even Luigi had to think about that question for a moment. But Luisa got it right away.

"What you know, Elwood, is all about Mr. Ling. You see, we don't know much about him."

"Except he'll shoot you with one of his quills," Luigi added.

Luisa shook her head at Luigi as if to say, *This is hard enough without extra comments like that, brother.*

As might be expected, Luigi's comment further confused Elwood. The sloth said, "Those quills hurt, too. I know. He shot two into me once. Sometimes I think he's just a mean porcupine."

He pondered a minute, and then he added, "Do you know if all porcupines are mean quill shooters? I only know Mr. Ling. Most of the time he's not mean. But sometimes he shoots quills. And you better run for cover when that happens."

Well, that was a mouthful for Elwood. More words than the twins had heard him say before. And to their amazement, what he said made sense.

Sort of.

But, by now the twins had lost Elwood's train of thought with the quill comment from Luigi. So, to make amends, Luigi took up the questioning again.

"Listen carefully, Elwood," Luigi said. "What you know that we need to know to find Mr. Ling is this: If he were to go somewhere to hide, where would he go?"

Elwood, considering Luigi's question, said, "I'm really thirsty. And hungry, too. Mr. Ling promised me a big lunch when I got back. But he left. He forgot me."

"Do you like chocolate cake and ice cream?" Luisa said.

"It's my favorite. And I like snakes, too," Elwood said.

Luigi grabbed the phone to call room service. He spoke quietly so neither Luisa nor Elwood could hear. Then, with a louder, "Thank you, Room Service," he announced, "Chocolate cake, ice cream and Pepsi-Cola for three are on the way. Fifteen minutes, Room Service said."

Elwood said, "That's good."

Then, out of nowhere, he added, "I know," and stared with some satisfaction at Luigi and Luisa.

Seizing on the unlikely thought that Elwood's brain had caught up with a question posed several minutes ago, Luigi said, "What do you know, Elwood?"

A huge smile crossed the sloth's face. "I know where Mr. Ling likes to go to hide. There are four places. He will be at one of them."

"Are they nearby?" Luisa asked.

"One is," Elwood answered.

"What about the other three?" Luigi said.

"They're far, far away. But I know where they are. I've been to all of them with Mr. Ling. I carry his suitcase, mostly. Or Mr. Ar-Chee's."

Meanwhile, in the Hotel's Security Office

While the twins continued what seemed to Buzzer a rather long questioning of Elwood in the Beijing Suite on the hotel's 4th floor, everybody else had come together in a conference room in the offices of the Hotel's security chief.

Under continued questioning, the mysterious woman refused still to give her name. Finally, Dusty had taken No Way into a separate room to try to get a name from him.

"That mysterious woman who works for you, Mr. No . . . what is her name?" Dusty asked.

No Way said, "Is she in trouble?"

"We don't know yet. But if she won't give her name—or you won't—then she will definitely be in trouble," Dusty said.

"Oh," No Way said. "In that case her name is Madam Name."

"Madam Name?" Dusty seemed exasperated. "She's Chinese, Mr. No. That name is not a Chinese name. How can that be?"

No Way looked thoughtful. "Well, that's what we call her. But I left off her last name. I believe you would call it surname in English. Right?"

Dusty, tired of playing games, said, "Yes, that's right. So, what is it?"

"No," No Way said. "Madam No Name. She's my third cousin."

"You wouldn't be playing games with me, would you, No Way?" Dusty said.

"No way! I said I would help," No Way said firmly. "There's no way I would play games with you."

He looked pensive. Then he went on, " I'm not safe until Ling Ting Tong is caught, am I?"

"Probably not, Mr. No," Dusty said. "Will Madam No Name confirm that's her name when we ask her?"

"Probably not," No Way said. "She's a terrible liar."

"Why do you want a terrible liar working for you?" Dusty asked, wondering if she'd missed something about the Chinese culture that might explain this strange puzzle.

No Way answered, "Of course I don't like her lies. But everybody has to have a job. That's the way it is in China. Everybody has a job. And every job is important."

Do you think Elwood really knows where Ling Ting Tong hides out? Will he tell Luigi and Luisa? Will all three of them get to enjoy their chocolate cake, ice cream, and Pepsi-Cola's? Where do you think the faraway places Mr. Ling hides might be? And what about the mysterious woman? Is she really a big-time liar? And is her name really Madam No Name? Where will the cats of the CIA and Cincinnati the dancing pig go first to try to find Ling Ting Tong?

* A Sloth in Time *

让我们来学习一些普通话[1]

By Luigi and Luisa

Imagine that, like us, you are in China. What would you call the members of your family? And what if you needed to see a doctor? Or talk to a policeman? What would you call them? Here are some names to help you.

English	Mandarin	Say it Like This
Mother	妈妈	Ma- ma
Father	爸爸	Ba\ ba
Brother	兄弟	Xiong- di\
Sister	姐妹	Jie^ mei\
Grandmother	祖母	Zu^ mu^
Grandfather	祖父	Zu^ fu\
Uncle	叔叔	Shu- shu
Aunt	阿姨	A yi/
Male cousin	堂兄弟	Tang/ xiong- di\
Female cousin	堂姐妹	Tang/ jie^ mei\
Doctor	医生	Yi- sheng-
Nurse	护士	Hu\ shi\
Hospital	医院	Yi- yuan\
Pharmacist	药剂师	Yao\ ji - shi-
Policeman	警察	Jing^ cha/
Cab driver	出租车司机	Chu- zu- che- si- ji-
Waitperson	伺应	Si\ ying\
Pilot	飞机师	Fei- ji- shi-
Flight attendant	空姐	Kong- jie^
Shopkeeper	店主	Dian\ zhu^
Guide	导游	Dao^ you/

---

1. Let's Learn to Speak Some Mandarin

Chapter Fourteen
The Chase is On
Beijing Suite—4th Floor—Peninsula Hotel

Buzzer and Cincinnati had decided that No Way and Madam No Name should be held on a short leash. Madam No to keep her from contacting Ling Ting Tong. And No Way to protect him from the anger of Mr. Ling. So they sent them both back to their offices at Mao's Mausoleum in Tiananmen Square where they would be guarded until the portly porcupine could be caught. Two of No Quil's agents would stay with them around the clock until it became safe for them to be released.

No Quil had decided that no charges would be filed against them if the porcupine could be brought to justice. He had also decided the time had come to bring in extra help. "I can't do this job alone," he'd said.

So he appealed to his bosses—Geng Huichang, Minister of State Security, and Wu Aying, Minister of Justice of the People's Republic of China. Both had agreed to send additional agents to whatever locations No Quil thought they might be needed. And those extra agents were now on standby, awaiting directions.

Buzzer, Cincinnati, Dusty and No Quil, their business with the hotel's security chief finished, had returned to the CIA cats' suite on the 4th floor. There, Luigi and Luisa waited for them to report on their game-playing conversation with Elwood, the slow-witted sloth.

With Luigi and Elwood still chatting in the suite's bedroom, Luisa began the report. "The most important thing to remember," she said, "is that Elwood thinks he will be playing a special new kind of hide and seek. We've told him that Ling Ting Tong has gone to hide where he thinks we will never find him. And

Elwood has said he's sure he knows where the porcupine will be hiding."

"Where?" Buzzer said.

Luisa said, "One of four places. One is right here in Beijing, and the other three, according to Elwood, are far, far away."

"Did he tell you where these places are?" Cincinnati asked.

"Yes," Luisa said. "And here they are. In Beijing, Elwood says Ling Ting Tong's favorite place to hide is in the Forbidden City— in the Hall of Supreme Harmony. It's right in the middle of the Forbidden City. Elwood says Ling Ting Tong often goes there to meditate. And, when the authorities are looking for him, that's where he hides. Elwood said Mr. Ling will go there first, and if he finds out we're looking for him anywhere around there, he will head south. Out of town."

"Okay," Buzzer said, "We'll start there. But we need to be prepared if he leaves Beijing and heads south as Elwood predicts. Did you find out where to the south he might go?"

"Luigi's in the bedroom now with Elwood showing him how a laptop computer works. But what he's really doing is researching the three locations Elwood gave us. Elwood thinks Luigi's magic—to be able to show pictures of all Ling Ting Tong's hiding places."

"So, where are they?" Cincinnati said with a touch of impatience.

"I'll let Elwood tell you," she said. "And Luigi can fill in the details. But, remember, he thinks this is a hide and seek game. And he thinks Luigi's laptop is a secret weapon to help us find Ling Ting Tong."

"It is," Dusty said. "It most certainly is."

"I'll get them," Luisa said, heading for the closed bedroom door. "But let Luigi and me do all the talking to Elwood. Elwood trusts Luigi and me, and he thinks we're going to have a lot of fun together."

Luigi and Elwood joined the rest of the group in the suite's parlor. Luigi ceremoniously introduced Buzzer, Cincinnati, Dusty and No Quil as the members of the team Elwood would lead in the game of hide and seek as they looked for Ling Ting Tong.

Luigi said, "Elwood, as the leader, it's your job to tell the rest of the team where you think we should look for Mr. Ling. Will you do that now, please?"

As an aside to the group, Luisa whispered, "Elwood speaks slowly. And sometimes it takes a minute or two for him to get his thoughts together. So please be patient. And let Luigi lead the conversation."

Elwood stood and, sipping a can of Pepsi, began to answer. "First, Mr. Ling will go to the Hall of Supreme Harmony in the Forbidden City." Then he stopped talking as if that might be all he intended to say.

So Luigi asked, "Where he would go after that—if he thought we were looking for him in the Forbidden City?"

"Far, far away," Elwood said, glancing out the window as if looking for far, far away.

Luisa asked, "Where is the first place he would go, Elwood. After the Hall of Supreme Harmony?"

It's far away," Elwood said.

"We know that. Thank you, Elwood. But where is that place." Thinking of a better way to ask the question, Luigi said, "What is the name of the next place?"

"You mean after the Hall of Supreme Harmony?" Elwood said, still confused.

"Yes, Elwood. After the Hall of Supreme Harmony."

"It's a Holiday Inn far away," Elwood said. "Sometimes we would meet Mr. Ar-Chee there."

Luisa said, "And in what city is this Holiday Inn?"

"I have to think real hard," Elwood said. "I told you before. What did I say then?"

Luigi answered, "You said in Hefei. Is that right? Is the city with the Holiday Inn called Hefei?"

Elwood's face lit up. "Yes, that's right. Like I said before, it's in Hefei."

Luisa whispered again to the rest of the group, "Don't worry, we have all the locations recorded, and Luigi and I have made a file on each one. But we have to keep Elwood thinking he's the leader. And it's his job to provide all the information to the team."

∗ The Chase is On ∗

"And if he leaves Hefei, Elwood, where would he go next?" Luigi asked.

Luigi continued the questions while Dusty began to fidget. Her impatience was about to make her scream at the pace of the questioning. Noticing that, Buzzer took her aside and reminded her that Elwood might be their best source for finding Ling Ting Tong. "He's a little slow-witted," Buzzer said, "but the twins are getting the information we need. Stay calm."

Trying to wind up this long questioning, Luigi began to drop hints. "And after Hefei, you said he would go to Guangzhou, right?"

"That's right." Elwood's recollection seemed faster than his pondering.

"To the White Swan Hotel in Guangzhou?" Luigi asked.

"Yes," Elwood said, "The White Swan. We went there lots of times to meet Mr. Ar-Chee. It's a big hotel. Very big."

"And finally," Luigi said, "where is the last place Ling Ting Tong might go?"

"I know, I know!" Elwood said. "To Hong Kong. We went there most of all."

"Do you remember where you stayed in Hong Kong? In what hotel?"

Elwood frowned, and then grimaced. The name of the hotel was escaping him.

"Would it have been a big hotel with a subway in the basement?" Luisa prompted. "Maybe the J.W. Marriott Hotel?"

"That's it! Elwood said. "Whatever you just said. That hotel."

Buzzer looked at Cincinnati with surprise. The basement of the J.W. Marriott Hotel in Hong Kong was where the two of them had captured Ar-Chee three years ago—before anyone even knew he would be in the opium smuggling business in years to come.

Buzzer stepped forward. "Elwood, you are a true leader. The information you've just given us will be very helpful in finding Mr. Ling. And that's what this new kind of hide and seek is all about. Finding Mr. Ling."

Cincinnati suggested Elwood should take a nap after working so hard. Elwood, full of chocolate cake and ice cream and Pep-

✴ Beijing Ding-a-Ling: Mao of the CIA ✴

si Cola, agreed. He shuttled off to the bedroom while Luigi and Luisa began to go over their files on the four locations Ling Ting Tong would likely go.

"Pull up a chair around the table, Luigi said. "And soon you'll know what Luisa and I have already figured out."

Dusty rolled her eyes.

But she said nothing.

No Quil grabbed his phone to call for agents to make their way to the Holiday Inn in Hefei, The White Swan Hotel in Guangzhou, and the J.W. Marriott Hotel in Hong Kong. He closed his conversation by saying, "Do not attempt to capture him, Just keep him in sight until we can get there. Capturing porcupines is my job—with the help of this team from the United States."

Do you think Ling Ting Tong is hiding in the Hall of Supreme Harmony in the Forbidden City? Or maybe in one of the hotels Elwood named in Hefei, Guangzhou or Hong Kong? What if Elwood is just making all this up—and he really doesn't know anything at all about where Mr. Ling might hide? What will the Cats of the CIA and Cincinnati the dancing pig do then? And how much will Luigi and Luisa already know about each of Ling Ting Tong's supposed hiding places?

* The Chase is On *

让我们来学习一些普通话[1]

By Luigi and Luisa

We're in Beijing in August—in the summertime. What if we came in the middle of the winter when it gets very, very cold here? How would we know what to wear? How would you know what to call the clothes you would need to bring? Here are some words to help you:

English	Mandarin	Say it Like This
Blouse	女式衬衫	Nv^ shi\ chen\shan-
Skirt	裙子	Qun^ zi
Slip	背心内衣	Bei\ xin- nei| yi
Shirt	衬衣	Chen\ yi
Pants	裤子	Ku\ zi
Belt	皮带	Pi/ dai\
Sweater	毛衣	Mao/ yi
Jacket	夹克	Jia/ ke\
Coat	大衣	Da\ yi
Hat	帽子	Mao\ zi
Cap	鸭舌帽	Ya- she/ mao\
Shoes	鞋子	Xie/ zi
Socks	袜子	Wa\ zi
Raincoat	雨衣	Yu^ yi
Umbrella	雨伞	Yu/ san
Gloves	手套	Shou ^ tao\
Mittens	毛线手套	Mao/ xian\ shou^ tao\
Parka	长大衣	Chang/ da\ yi
Boots	靴子	Xue- zi
Galoshes	胶鞋	Jiao- xie/

---
1. Let's Learn to Speak Some Mandarin

Chapter Fifteen
First Stop: Close to Home

Beijing Suite—4th Floor—Peninsula Hotel

Dusty wondered how the twins had amassed such a big file on Ling Ting Tong's likely hiding places. After all, they'd had only a couple of hours to question Elwood the sloth. Then again, she thought, *I guess I shouldn't be surprised. Those two can be amazing when they get busy. And they sure have been busy today.*

Luigi and Luisa took turns briefing the team on the four likely locations that Mr. Ling might flee to. They took care to be specific and include an unusual amount of detail about each place. When they had finished, Dusty Louise asked, "How can we be sure this Elwood knows what he's talking about? He's not too bright, you know. Maybe he's just saying the first thing that comes to his mind . . . if anything at all comes to his mind."

Luigi looked at Luisa. She shrugged, then said, "Go."

So Luigi began. "Luisa and I have learned—and practiced—the many ways to question a suspect, Dusty. It's an art. And if you don't know how to do it properly, just what you described is likely to happen. That is, bad information will come out that will cause us to go off on several wrong directions at once."

"Wild-goose chases," Luisa added.

Cincinnati turned to Buzzer and nodded. Quickly Buzzer said, "Tell us about these secrets of questioning. And how you used them to be sure the information you've gotten from Elwood is reliable."

Buzzer's question was exactly what the twins had hoped somebody would ask. Luigi stood tall, puffed out his chest, and saluted his big brother. That let everyone know he and Luisa were about to say some important things.

Luisa began, "Here's the way it works. The two of us operate as a team. Our first job is to gain the confidence of the one we're about to question. In Elwood's case, that wasn't too hard."

Luigi added, "Very easy, as a matter of fact. Because Elwood is slow-witted, he's really never had anybody take an interest in him. Personally, I mean. He's usually the butt of jokes. Or just ignored completely."

Luisa went on, "So Luigi and I just became his friends by being kind, asking him about himself, and taking a personal interest in Elwood, the sloth. That had rarely, if ever, happened to him before."

"Soon, he became comfortable talking with us," Luigi said. "He could see that we not only liked talking with him, but also we found what he had to say interesting. And important."

Luisa continued the explanation. "So we began to turn the conversation slowly into the questions we really needed the answers to. It didn't take long for us to see that Elwood really did have some valuable information to help us find Mr. Ling. We learned quickly that Elwood had worked with Ar-Chee and Ling Ting Tong for several years. And in that time, he had traveled all over the place with them."

"Actually," Luigi said, "he'd just followed along with them doing simple chores. But it was clear he could remember where he had been . . . and how Mr. Ling, in particular, had behaved when he needed to hide out for a while."

Luisa went on. "So we asked him questions. They seemed to him to be just random questions because he's not very well organized mentally—if you know what I mean. I would ask him a question, and then a few minutes later Luigi would ask the same question. But in a slightly different way. What we found was that Elwood's answers were consistent. If he didn't remember—or didn't know—he wouldn't guess. Or give us any kind of answer."

Luigi said, "That told us, along with the consistency of his answers to the same questions, that we could expect that what he was telling us was likely true. And accurate."

Luisa finished the explanation with a flourish. "So that's how we came to believe that what we were learning from Elwood would most certainly be worth looking into. And acting on."

Luigi said, "Any questions?"

Buzzer beamed at the twins while Cincinnati slowly clapped his two front hooves together. Cincinnati asked, "And where did you two learn these questioning techniques?"

Buzzer added, "Yes, I'd like to know too. They're taught, just as you described them, in every criminal justice school I've ever heard of. But I know neither of you has been to any of those classes. Not yet, anyway."

Luisa scratched her chin and looked serious. "Buzzer and Cincinnati, have you ever heard of a detective named Sherlock Holmes?"

"And his assistant, Dr. Watson?" Luigi added. "That's the way they question suspects."

Luisa added, "And they always know if the information they're getting is truthful. Or a lie."

Buzzer smiled and said, "Good work."

Dusty, ever suspicious of the twins, said, "So you're absolutely sure we can count on the information Elwood has provided to help us find Ling Ting Tong?"

Luigi and Luisa looked at one another. They both shrugged. Luisa answered. "Absolutely sure? No. We can't be absolutely sure. We've done our best to get good information from Elwood. And, for the most part, we believe it to be useful. Strongly believe it to be useful."

Luigi jumped in, "But absolutely sure? No, Dusty, not absolutely sure"

"But we do know one thing for sure. Absolutely," Luisa said.

"What's that?" Dusty asked.

"We are absolutely sure it is the only real information we have. China is a big country. And there are only a few of us. We can ignore what we think we know. And try to find a porcupine quill in a haystack."

"Or," Luigi added, "we can use the best information we have and follow the path Elwood believes Mr. Ling will take. A path Elwood's seen him take before."

Dusty smiled. "When you put it that way, I can see we real-

∗ First Stop: Close to Home ∗

ly have no choice. So, do you have a plan ready for us? I can't imagine how you could have one so quickly. But you continue to amaze me."

Once again, Luigi stood and saluted. "Yes, we have a plan. And here it is."

Luisa began, "Luigi and I will take responsibility for the Hall of Supreme Harmony right here in the Forbidden City. We've had time to get up to speed on it as a hiding place. With Elwood's help, of course. It's the first place we need to look. And we need to get over there right away. If Mr. Ling is hiding there, maybe we can catch him before he decides to run farther away from Beijing."

Luigi continued, "And Mr. No Quil, will you please be responsible for the Holiday Inn in Hefei? You have agents on their way there. None of us has ever visited there, so you will know more about it than we do. Here's the file." Luigi handed No Quil the information the twins had gathered on Hefei and the particular Holiday Inn there with the revolving restaurant on the top. Another place Mr. Ling had been known to hide out.

Luisa handed Dusty Louise a file. She said, "This is the file on the White Swan Hotel in Guangzhou. Dusty, we need you to be the leader of this search. It's a famous place, so you won't have a problem finding out a lot more information about it."

Luigi added, "And don't forget, No Quil has agents on the way there right now. Work with them. And keep us all posted. Thank you, Dusty."

"Finally," Luigi said, "we all hope to catch Mr. Ling long before we have to go to Hong Kong. But if we do have to go there, who better knows the J.W. Marriott in Hong Kong than Buzzer and Cincinnati? After all, you have both stayed there before. You actually trapped Ar-Chee there. Here's our file . . . what we've discovered so far."

No Quil, the Chinese assistant director of porcupine catching, spoke up. "Excellent work, Luigi and Luisa. We will find this Mr. Ling. And we will bring him to justice. I have the commitment and backing of the government of the People's Republic of China behind us. So let's get about it!"

※ Beijing Ding-a-Ling: Mao of the CIA ※

Luigi said, "Yes, let's get on with it. We'll begin with a brief review of the information we covered earlier about the Hall of Supreme Harmony. Luisa and I have specific assignments for each of you as we approach it. Right now, Luisa will hit the high points."

Luisa grabbed a marker and walked up to a white board they'd been using. As she began to draw a bird's-eye diagram of the Hall in the Outer Court of the Forbidden City, she reviewed the high points of the file.

"This building has been in place for more than 600 years. But it has been destroyed seven times by fire. The current structure was rebuilt about 320 years ago. And it's the largest wooden structure in China. Over the centuries, it was used for royal weddings, inaugurations, and ceremonies of all types. Emperors often held discussions of affairs of their country there."

Again, Dusty asked, "What's so special about it except it's big and made of wood?"

Luigi grinned. "There are paintings and sculptures of dragons all around inside the building."

Do you think Elwood the sloth really knows what he's talking about? Will our heroes find Ling Ting Tong by following the plan Luigi and Luisa have developed? Why do you think the Hall of Supreme Harmony is built of wood? Especially after it burned seven times? Will Ling Ting Tong be in the Forbidden City? Or will he have escaped Beijing and headed farther south? Will the Cats of the CIA and No Quil take Elwood along with them? Or will they leave him napping in the Beijing suite of the Peninsula Hotel?

* First Stop: Close to Home *

让我们来学习一些普通话[1]

By Luigi and Luisa

In our line of work, even though it's mostly done in secret, you can see that we have to deal with a lot of different characters—both human and animals. Lots of different kinds of animals. Here are the names of some animals for you to use when you are in China. Or you wish to speak Mandarin.

English	Mandarin	Say it like This
Cat	猫	Mao-
Porcupine	刺猬	Ci\ wei\
Panda bear	熊猫	Xiong/ mao-
Dog	狗	Gou^
Horse	马	Ma^
Cow	牛	Niu/
Goat	山羊	Shan-yang/
Sheep	绵羊	Mian/ yang/
Pig	猪	Zhu-
Sloth	树懒	Shu\ lan^
Fox	狐狸	Hu/ li/
Wolf	狼	Lang/
Chicken	鸡	Ji-
Duck	鸭	Ya-
Bird	鸟	Niao^
Monkey	猴子	Hou/ zi
Snake	蛇	She/
Fish	鱼	Yu/
Lion	狮子	Shi- zi
Tiger	老虎	Lao^ hu^
Elephant	大象	Da\ xiang\
Puma	豹	Bao\
Camel	骆驼	Luo\tuo/

---

1. Let's Learn to Speak Some Mandarin

* Beijing Ding-a-Ling: Mao of the CIA *

Chapter Sixteen
Double Trouble
Hall of Supreme Harmony—Forbidden City

As they stepped through the Meridian Gate that opened to the Outer Court of the Forbidden City, the Hall of Supreme Harmony loomed before them.

Luisa spoke up. "That's it," she said. "The big building straight ahead. It's the largest single building in the Forbidden City."

Luigi piped up, "Yes, it's 210 feet wide and 122 feet deep and about 35 feet tall. So it covers almost two-thirds of an acre. But it's mostly open, so we won't have too much trouble seeing if Mr. Ling is in there."

Their plan included having the twins move straight to the center of the great hall by the Emperor's Imperial Dragon Throne while Cincinnati and No Quil checked the outside perimeter and Dusty and Buzzer began their search by looking carefully around the inside walls. They were all to meet in the center by the throne with five dragons carved into it.

The crowds were fairly small, so the searchers were able to make their rounds quickly.

As the team moved back toward the Dragon Throne, No Quil's phone rang. He stopped, answered it, listened for a moment, then clicked off and hurried to meet the others.

"He's not here," No Quil said.

"Can we be sure?" Dusty asked. "Maybe we should go around again."

"No! He's not here!" No Quil insisted.

"How do you know that?" Cincinnati asked.

"Because Ar-Chee just escaped from his cell at Qincheng Prison. With the help of his lawyer—a porcupine who spoke several languages to the guards."

"Ling Ting Tong!" Luigi shouted. "And now they're both on the loose."

Luisa added, "And they're together. Double trouble for us."

No Quil shook his head. "This just can't be possible. Nobody has ever escaped from that prison. It's maximum security."

Cincinnati said, "Apparently not maximum enough." He paused, seeming to be thinking. Then he said, "So, where do we go from here?"

Luigi answered instantly. "Back to our rooms at the Peninsula Hotel. We need to ask a few more questions to Elwood. And we need to talk to Socks. And maybe even Boris in Russia. We need more information."

Luisa spoke up. "Let's not get in a tizzy, here," she said. "Luigi and I have a Plan E. We always have a Plan E because you never know what might happen to Plans A through D."

"What's your Plan E?" Dusty said challengingly.

Luigi answered, "As the Sloth Turns."

Peninsula Hotel—Beijing Suite—4th Floor

No Quil left the group and went to his office to check with his teams of agents in Hefei, Guangzhou, and Hong Kong. He wanted to let them know that their target now included a large panda as well as a portly porcupine.

As the rest of the group returned to the Beijing Suite, they found Elwood in a strange mood. He paced back and forth, mumbling to himself. He seemed to not even notice that the group had returned. As he continued pacing, glancing out the windows and mumbling. Luigi and Luisa moved to stand in front of him, almost tripping him.

"What's up, Elwood?" Luigi asked. "Why are you in such a dither?"

The sloth, unable to speak, reached into his pocket. He pulled out a piece of paper and handed it to Luisa. He spoke but one word. "Look!"

Luisa glanced at the paper, said it appeared to be a note from Mr. Ling, and then set it on a table for everyone to see.

Elwood,

Good news! We are back in business. And, of course, we need your help. You know we can't get anything done without you.

Join us at the usual place tomorrow afternoon at three o'clock. Call us when you get there.

Your friends,
Ar-Chee and Ling Ting Tong

Where would the usual place be? Do you think Luigi and Luisa's Plan E might include getting some more help from Elwood? What do you think they'll want him to do this time? Will it be harder to capture two smugglers than just one? Remember that Ar-Chee is not very smart. But can Luisa and Luigi make Elwood smart enough to lead them to the panda and the porcupine?

* Beijing Ding-a-Ling: Mao of the CIA *

让我们来学习一些普通话[1]

By Luigi and Luisa

What would you do if you became ill or hurt yourself while you were in China? You would need to know how to tell a doctor or a pharmacist where you're hurt. And that means knowing how to say the various parts of your body. Here are some words to learn. Just in case.

English	Mandarin	**Say it Like This**
Hair	头发	Tou/ fa
Head	头	Tou/
Ear	耳	Er^
Nose	鼻子	Bi/ zi
Eye	眼睛	Yan^jing-
Chin	下巴	Xia\ ba
Neck	颈	Jing^
Shoulder	肩膀	Jian-bang^
Arm	手臂	Shou^ bi\
Elbow	手弯头	Shou^ wan tou/
Wrist	手腕	Shou^ wan^
Hand	手	Shou^
Fingers	手指	Shou^ zhi
Chest	胸脯	Xiong- pu/
Stomach	胃	Wei\
Heart	心脏	Xin- zang\
Hip	臀部	Tun/ bu\
Thigh	大腿	Da\ tui^
Knee	膝盖	xi- gai\
Shin	外脚小腿	Wai\ jiao^ xiao^ tui^

---

1. Let's Learn to Speak Some Mandarin

Chapter Seventeen
As the Sloth Turns
Beijing Suite—Peninsula Hotel

After a brief private discussion among the team members, Luigi and Luisa had led Elwood to one of the bedrooms. Their plan included convincing the sloth that he could become a national hero in the People's Republic of China. The first sloth in history to be honored by the inhabitants of a single country. And, in this case, the most populated country in the world.

Knowing that Elwood not only trusted Luisa, but also really liked her, Luigi suggested she begin their conversation.

"Elwood," she began, "are you proud to be a sloth?"

Elwood frowned. "That's what I am," he said. "Should I be proud of that?"

"What do you think?" Luisa said. "What if you were a kangaroo? Or a penguin, maybe?" Luisa could tell she had confused Elwood. Which is exactly what she'd intended to do. "So, what do you think, Elwood?" she asked again.

Elwood clearly seemed perplexed. He scratched his chin, squinted, and furrowed his brow. Then he said, "I guess one of those—a kangaroo or a penguin—might be okay. But I don't know how to be either one of them." He thought hard, and then added, "But I do know how to be a sloth."

A bright smile crossed his face.

Luigi spoke up, "You know, Elwood, the world gives very little thought to sloths. And even less credit. Have you ever heard of a famous sloth?"

Again Elwood thought hard. "No," he said, "I don't think there has ever been a famous sloth. Do you?"

Luisa said, "No, Elwood. There has never been a famous

* Beijing Ding-a-Ling: Mao of the CIA *

sloth."

Luigi added, "In fact, sloths are always looked down upon by other creatures. Everyone thinks of them as lazy. Shiftless. Mostly worthless. Did you know that, Elwood? Sloths are known the world over as lazy bums."

Elwood's eyes sparkled. "My grandmother told me all about that when I was a baby. She said I would never be respected as an individual except by other sloths. And that even three-toed sloths would look down on me because I have only two toes."

Luisa looked sympathetic. "And have you learned to live with this lack of respect, Elwood?"

The sloth looked down, staring at the floor. He said, "It's hard sometimes. Only Ar-Chee and Mr. Ling have ever been nice to me. Nobody else pays me any attention. If they even notice me at all."

"Ah, yes," Luigi said. "The life of a sloth is not easy, is it?"

"No, it's not," Elwood said, as a tear trickled down his cheek. "But it's what I am. Nothing I can do about it."

Luisa stepped in front of Elwood. She smiled, "Maybe there is something you can do, Elwood. And maybe Luigi and I can help you do it."

Luigi added, speaking slowly, "How would you like to become a big hero, Elwood? How would you like to be honored as one of the most important inhabitants in all of China?"

Elwood's expression went from dubious to doubtful to interested to intrigued as Luigi kept feeding possibilities to him.

Luigi continued, "What if you could be on the front page of every newspaper in China. On television, too. And meet with the premier and all the top officials of the government? What if they called for a national holiday to celebrate the heroic deeds of Elwood the sloth?"

"Think of it, Elwood," Luisa stepped in. "You can be the first sloth ever to be a national hero. Sloth Day will replace Groundhog Day. Everyone will celebrate sloths for the first time. Nobody will ever again label anyone else 'slothful.' No, they'll be 'groundhogful,' instead. And sloths will be celebrated all over the world."

Luigi added, "All because a two-toed sloth in Beijing did

something so special. So heroic. So important to the world that he changed the attitude about and lives of all sloths Everywhere. Forever."

"How does that sound to you, Elwood?" Luisa said.

Still beaming at the possibilities, Elwood said, "That would be great. But who can we get to be this hero?"

Luisa batted her eyelashes and said softly, "You, Elwood. You. Luigi and I can help you. We'll show you what to do. Stick with us, Elwood. And you can be that hero."

Back in the Suite's Parlor

While Luigi and Luisa worked with Elwood in the bedroom, Buzzer, Dusty and Cincinnati made some phone calls.

First Buzzer had called Dr. Buford Lewis, the foreman of his little ranch in the Texas Hill Country. Buford, a Labrador retriever and professor emeritus at the University of California at Barkley, and his very smart brother, Bogart-BOGART, looked after the little ranch when Buzzer and the team were out of town. Which had been almost all the time for the past three months.

Learning that all remained well with the ranch and Dr. Buford and Bogart-BOGART, Buzzer then called Socks, their boss, in the basement of the White House.

Socks's phone rang.

She answered, "You have reached the number you have dialed. To whom do you wish to speak, please?"

"Socks, it's me—Buzzer Louis."

"Buzzer, I knew that. You missed my try at a little humor."

Cincinnati said, "You better leave the humor to Luigi and Luisa. Maybe we missed it because it wasn't really there, Socks."

Dusty, ever impatient, broke in. "Stop fooling around, all of you! We have serious work to do here. There's no time for all this folderol."

Buzzer said into the phone, "Well, Socks, Dusty has spoken. So let's get down to business. No more folderol. We need some help. Or at least we will need some help when Luigi and Luisa finish prepping Elwood."

"Who's Elwood?" Socks asked. "I thought you were working with an assistant minister named No Quil."

"We are," Buzzer said. "Maybe I better start from the beginning. Ar-Chee has escaped from prison. Apparently Ling Ting Tong posed as his attorney and somehow sneaked him out of Qincheng Prison."

Socks said, "You're kidding. Nobody has ever escaped from that terrible prison before. How did they do that?"

Buzzer said, "We don't know. But that's not the point. They're out, and the two of them are on the loose, ready to start up their opium smuggling once again."

Socks waited patiently while Buzzer collected his thoughts. Then Buzzer continued. "That brings the story to the subject of Elwood . . ."

Buzzer then told Socks about Elwood and his job as a faithful helper for Ar-Chee and Mr. Ling. He explained that Luigi and Luisa had made a friend of Elwood, and at the moment they were in another room with the sloth working on their Plan E to capture both the panda and the porcupine.

Socks wanted to know, "What happened to Plans A through D? And what is their Plan E?"

Cincinnati answered, "We're not sure. In fact, Socks, all we really know is the name they've given the plan."

"And what's that?" Socks asked.

Dusty answered, "As the Sloth Turns."

Back in the Bedroom with Elwood

The twins had spent some time encouraging Elwood. The sloth had been concerned about his loyalty to Mr. Ling, in particular. Helping him see that what Ar-Chee and Mr. Ling continued to do was a bad thing. Elwood finally came around. But only after the twins promised he would not have to directly betray Mr. Ling.

"We'll take care of that," Luisa had reassured him. "You just work with us, Elwood. We'll make you a hero."

A call to No Quil had sealed the sloth's cooperation. The twins had convinced No Quil, assistant minister of porcupine catching, to hire Elwood as his assistant. After the celebrations, of course.

With a little encouragement from Luigi and Luisa, No Quil told Elwood, "You help me catch this porcupine and the panda, and I will not only share the credit with you, but I'll also tell the world that without your help, these villains might never have been caught."

He paused a moment and then went on. "My boss will personally introduce you to Hu Jintao, our premier. You'll be a hero, and you will have an important job forever. Doing good things, Elwood, instead of helping criminals."

To make the whole agreement official, Luigi had produced a sharp pin. He, Luisa and Elwood had each squeezed out a tiny drop of blood and then mixed the three drops.

"Now we're blood brothers and sisters," Luisa had said. "Nothing will get in the way of our plan."

This time Elwood spoke up, "We will catch the bad guys. And I will become a hero. To honor sloths forever."

We know Elwood isn't really very smart. Do you think he understands what he's agreed to do? Will he help the Cats of the CIA and No Quil catch Ar-Chee and Mr. Ling? If he does, will he really become a national hero? The first sloth hero ever? Anywhere? And will No Quil share the credit with Elwood to help him become a hero? What do you think Elwood will say to Premier Hu Jintao? Finally, where do you think Ling Ting Tong meant when he asked Elwood to meet himself and Ar-Chee at "the usual place?"

Beijing Ding-a-Ling: Mao of the CIA

让我们来学习一些普通话[1]

By Luisa and Luigi

In every language, there are common, everyday words and phrases that we use over and over. Questions. Conversation starters. Greetings. Here are some that will be useful to you if you go to China or anywhere that Mandarin is spoken.

English	Mandarin	Say it Like This
Hello	你好	Ni^ hao^
Goodbye	再见	Zai\ jian\
My name is	我的名字是......	Wo ^ de ming/ zi shi\.......
What's your name?	你叫什么名字？	Ni^jiao\ shen me ming/ zi ?
Where is a telephone?	电话在哪里？	Dian\hua\ zai\ na/li ?
Where is the bathroom?	洗手间在哪里？	Xi^ shou^ jian- zai\ na/li
That's very pretty	那是非常漂亮	Na\ shi\ fei- chang/ piao\ liang\
Thank you	谢谢你	Xie\ xie\ ni
You're welcome	不客气	Bu/ ke\ qi\
How much does it cost?	这个多少钱？	Zhe\ ge\ duo- shao^ qian/
How are you?	你好吗？	Ni/ hao^ ma?
I feel fine	我很好	Wo^ hen/ hao^
What is the weather today?	今天天气怎样？	Jin- tian- tian-qi\ zen^ yang\?
Excuse me	打扰一下	Da^ rao^ yi- xia\
May I introduce you to	我能把你介绍给。。。	Wo^ neng/ ba^ ni jie\ shao\ gei^.....
Where do you live?	你住在哪里？	Ni^ zhu\ zai\ na^ li?
I'm sorry	我很抱歉	Wo^ hen^ bao/ qian\
I apologize	我为此道歉	Wo^ wei\ ci^ dao\ qian\
I do not speak Mandarin well	我的普通话说得不好	Wo^ de pu^ tong- hua\ shuo- de bu\ hao^

---

1. Let's Learn to Speak Some Mandarin

Chapter Eighteen
The Usual Place
The Beijing Suite—A Few Minutes Later

When the twins had finished preparing Elwood for his new role as the world's first hero sloth, they spent some time figuring out what "the usual place' meant in the note that had been left for him. They learned that Elwood's visual recognition and recall were both quite good. He could picture in his mind places he had been. But he had problems recalling names of cities and places.

As they were about to become frustrated, Luisa remembered the list of four places the sloth had given them just hours earlier. She and Luigi questioned Elwood on each place.

"It won't be the Hall of Supreme Harmony in the Forbidden City, will it?" she asked.

Elwood shook his head, saying only, "Farther away. Not Beijing."

Luigi asked, "What about Hefei. Remember the Holiday Inn with the revolving restaurant on top? Is that 'the usual place,' Elwood?"

Elwood frowned, scratched his chin, frowned some more, and said, "No. Not that place. It's a longer train ride away. Several hours by plane, too. Big, big city. Big, big hotel."

"Guangzhou?" Luisa asked. "The White Swan Hotel in Guangzhou?"

This time Elwood sat down. He thought for several minutes. Luigi and Luisa could tell he was concentrating, doing his best to remember the name of "the usual place" that he could see in his mind's eye.

Finally, he looked up, eyes bright, and said, "They have big breakfasts there. And there is a train in the basement."

* Beijing Ding-a-Ling: Mao of the CIA *

Luigi jumped up and saluted. "Hong Kong!" he said.

"The J.W. Marriott Hotel in Hong Kong," Luisa said, sure now that they knew where to find Ar-Chee and Ling Ting Tong tomorrow.

Downtown Hong Kong—The Next Morning, Early

Once the porcupine hunters had figured out where "the usual place" was, it was too late in the evening to catch a commercial flight to Hong Kong. Luigi and Luisa thought it very important not to arrive in broad daylight. That would happen if they took the first commercial flight in the morning.

No Quil came to the rescue. He arranged for two pilots and a Harbin Y-12 airplane from Geng Huichang, Chinese minister of state security--and No Quil's immediate boss. The plane was old and small, with 17 seats. But only seven porcupine chasers headed for Hong Kong. The plane, too, proved slower than Cincinnati's *The Flying Pig Machine*, taking almost four hours to fly the 1,250 miles from Beijing to Hong Kong.

Cincinnati, fascinated as usual with different kinds of flying machines, sat behind the pilots and soon figured out how to fly the Y-12. He whispered to Buzzer, "I'm not much impressed with this heap. It's slow. And watch the pilot. He's straining to keep us on course and level. If it were a bicycle, it would have only one wheel—a unicycle."

During the last half of their flight, the co-pilot talked about Hong Kong, in case his passengers might not know its history.

"Hong Kong has one of the finest natural harbors in the world," he said. "British and Dutch explorers discovered it hundreds of years ago, and it soon developed as a major trading center. More recently, Hong Kong was a British colony until a few years ago. When the agreement with the British ended before the turn of the twenty-first century, the territory was returned to the People's Republic of China. It's still a major seaport. And it has become one of the world's busiest financial and banking centers, too."

The private ride ended when their plane landed in Hong Kong at 5:30 in the morning. They thanked their pilots and climbed aboard a Ministry of Security SUV for the trip from the island airport into the city of Hong Kong.

"If Ar-Chee and Ling Ting Tong are going to be at the J.W. Marriott," Luigi said, "then we don't want to be there. If they should see us, any chance of surprising them would be lost."

Luisa said, "Yes, but they are expecting Elwood. And there's little chance they would know or recognize No Quil. I say let's use Elwood as a decoy and send No Quil into the hotel."

Dusty Louise said, "I suppose you two have already figured out a plan? A foolproof plan to catch these drug smugglers?"

Buzzer Louis answered her. "No plan can be completely foolproof, Dusty. Especially when one or more fools is involved. Mr. Ling is bright and clever. But surely Ar-Chee is often a fool. Anyway," he went on, "let's hear what the twins have in mind. They seem to have given the matter some serious thought."

Sitting down around a table in a small bistro in the basement of the big building that housed the J.W. Marriott Hotel, the group listened to the twins as they all sipped their morning coffee and milk.

Luigi and Luisa described their plan. While the plan seemed simple—not at all complicated—making it work would require splitting the group into three parts. And they would need to bring in the two agents that No Quil had dispatched yesterday to Hong Kong to watch for the porcupine, even before they knew Ar-Chee had escaped from prison.

The capture plan began with No Quil paying a visit to the maitre d' at the breakfast buffet upstairs in the hotel, followed shortly by a phone call to the two smugglers from Elwood.

At 7:30, No Quil left to speak to the maitre d'. Elwood, Luigi and Luisa left to catch the first cable car of the day to the top of Victoria Peak, a small, cone-shaped mountain with an observation deck that overlooked all of Hong Kong and its harbor. One of No Quil's agents shadowed the assistant minister of porcupine catching while the other went with Buzzer, Dusty and Cincinnati to rent a large SUV.

When the twins and Elwood had arrived at the top of Victoria Peak, They waited for their signal to start the capture plan. As they looked out over the city of skyscrapers and its beautiful and bustling harbor (Hong Kong means "Fragrant Harbor"), Luigi's satellite phone buzzed.

"Time to go!" Luigi said, punching in a number he'd memorized and handing the phone to Elwood.

Back in the Hotel's Dining Room

Ar-Chee and Ling Ting Tong had passed through the morning's massive buffet offerings and had sat down to eat their breakfasts. Ar-Chee had selected kippered herring, smoked salmon, and a fruit cup. Mr. Ling had chosen mostly berries and nuts. They both sipped café lattes.

As they began to eat, speaking very little to one another, the maitre d' approached with a cordless phone. He spoke to Ar-Chee.

"Excuse me, Sir," he said, "but there is a phone call for you." He handed the phone to the panda.

Ling Ting Tong objected. "How can there be a phone call for one of us?" he said. "No one knows where we are. This must be a mistake."

"Who did the caller ask to speak to?" Ar-Chee asked.

Mr. Ling corrected him, "That would be 'to whom did the caller ask to speak?'"

"What-ever," Ar-Chee said with disgust. He didn't much enjoy the porcupine correcting his grammar and syntax.

The maitre d' answered, "The caller, Sir, asked to speak to a large panda. He said the panda would most likely be accompanied by a portly porcupine."

"So you decided that would be us?" Ling Ting Tong asked indignantly.

"A mere deduction, Sir," the maitre d' answered. "Since you are the only panda and porcupine in the buffet at the moment." He looked at Ar-Chee. "Do you want to take the call, Sir? Or shall I tell the caller you refuse to speak to him?"

Ling Ting Tong, still puzzled, asked, "Did the caller identify himself?"

"He did, Sir. He said to tell you his name is Elwood."

"Elwood! Oh, sorry," Mr. Ling said. "Elwood knows where we are. My mistake."

"Very well, Sir," the maitre d' said, Rolling his eyes and walking away to return to his duties at the buffet line.

Ar-Chee answered. "Hello, Elwood. Where are you?"

At the Top of Victoria Peak

"Hi, Mr. Ar-Chee. I'm here in Hong Kong. That's where you wanted me. Right?"

Both Luigi and Luisa had encouraged Elwood to keep the conversation short. Too much talking might raise suspicions.

Ar-Chee said, "Are you at the hotel? If you are, come on down to the restaurant and join us for breakfast."

"No, Sir," Elwood said. "I'm in a little trouble." Luigi motioned for him to keep talking. "See, Mr. Ar-Chee, I rode the cable car up to the top of Victoria Peak to have my breakfast when the sun came up. But I forgot I don't have any money to ride it back down. Can you bring me some money, please? I don't want to stay up here all day. Thank you."

Ar-Chee answered, "We're just finishing our breakfast, Elwood. One of us will be there soon to rescue you. Sit tight."

"Which one?" Elwood said. "I mean, which one of you will come for me?"

"Does it matter?" Ar-Chee said.

"I hope it will be you," Elwood said. "Mr. Ling is going to be very mad at me."

"Don't worry. I'll come myself," Ar-Chee said.

Luigi motioned for Elwood to end the call. When the sloth seemed unable to move, frozen, Luisa grabbed the phone and clicked off.

Within minutes, the earpieces they all were wearing came to life. It was No Quil. "Ar-Chee just left the hotel. The bellman hailed a cab for him. He's headed for Victoria Peak."

Cincinnati, sitting in a rented SUV with Buzzer, one of No Quil's agents, and Dusty, said, "We're driving to the top now. We'll be there to meet him. Who's watching Ling Ting Tong?"

"I've got Mr. Ling in sight," No Quil said. "He's gone back to their suite. We're ready for him if he tries to leave."

Luigi couldn't keep from adding, "Separate them. That was the plan. Capture each one in a completely different place. It's working."

Is it working? Will the Cats of the CIA and No Quil be able, at last, to capture Ar-Chee at the top of Victoria Peak? And where will they capture Ling Ting Tong? In the hotel? What if the porcupine makes a run for it? Will No Quil and his assistant be able to stop him?

✳ **The Usual Place** ✳

让我们来学习一些普通话[1]

By Luigi and Luisa

We've covered a lot of ground in China so far. But it's a very big country with many interesting places to visit. Here are the names of some of China's major cities and attractions... and how to say them in Mandarin.

English	Mandarin	Say it Like This
Beijing	北京	Bei^ jing
Great Wall	长城	Chang/ cheng/
Qincheng Prison	秦城监狱	Qin/ cheng/ jiang- yu\
Hefei	合肥	He/ fei/
Shanghai	上海	Shang\ hai^
Guangzhou	广州	Guang^ zhou-
Hong Kong	香港	Xiang- gang^
Victoria Peak	维多利亚港	Wei/ duo- li\ ya\ gang^
Peninsula Hotel	半岛酒店	Ban\ dao^ jiu^ dian\
J.W. Marriott Hotel	金茂万豪酒店	Jin- mao/ wan\ hao/ jiu^ dian\
Fragrant harbor	香港	Xiang- gang^

---
1. Let's Learn to Speak Some Mandarin

Chapter Nineteen
A Fitting Finish
Hong Kong—J.W. Marriott Hotel

No Quil spoke into their radio communication system, "Ling Ting Tong just left his room. He called the bell captain and asked for a cab to take him to Victoria Peak. He must be worried that Ar-Chee is being set up."

"Can you follow that cab?" Cincinnati said. "Buzzer's driving us to the top of Victoria Peak as fast as we can go on this winding, twisty road. It's the only way up except for the cable cars."

No Quil answered, "I can do better than follow Mr. Ling. I'll be leading him. I'm driving the cab he's going to be riding in."

"Okay," Cincinnati said. "Your other agent is waiting at the bottom of the cable car tracks where we dropped him off. Send him up with Ling Ting Tong if the porcupine decides to ride to the top. By then, we should have Ar-Chee trapped up there. And take your time getting here. We don't want the two of them on the same cable car to the top."

Sure enough, the back door to the cab was opened by the bell captain. Ling Ting Tong climbed in and said, "Victoria cable-car lift, please."

No Quil answered, "On our way, Sir." He put the cab in gear and eased slowly out of the hotel's big portico into the morning traffic.

Hong Kong—Victoria Peak Observation Platform

Once again, the radio communication system broke its silence. It was No Quil's agent at the bottom. "Ar-Chee's just gotten into the cable car."

"Who else is in it with him?" Luigi asked.

* A Fitting Finish *

"So far, he's alone," the agent said.

"Then get the attendant to start it up," Luigi said. "But about halfway up, have him stop it until we signal you. We need to be sure Buzzer, Cincinnati and Dusty Louise are all here before that car gets to the top."

"Besides," Luisa added, "stopping the car halfway up will un-nerve Ar-Chee. Put him off his usual wariness and make him easier to catch. Just let it swing in the breeze until you hear from us."

In the Big SUV Driving to the Top of Victoria Peak

"Can we go any faster?" Dusty asked. "I don't want those twins alone up there with Ar-Chee. That sloth Elwood won't be much help to protect them."

"They won't be," Buzzer said. "The cable car won't be to the top until after we get there and get our nets rigged."

Cincinnati had brought along a big fishing net from a pier next to the car rental agency where they'd picked up the SUV an hour earlier. Their plan was to rig it over the opening into which the cable car would enter at the top. And then drop the net over Ar-Chee when he stepped out of the car.

"There's the observation deck!" Dusty Louise said as Buzzer pulled the SUV into a tiny parking lot at the top of Victoria Peak.

"Tell the bottom platform to let the cable car come on up," Cincinnati said to Dusty as he and Buzzer raced to meet the twins and Elwood and to stretch the net. The net that would trap Ar-Chee as he stepped out of the cable car and onto the platform at the top.

Back at the Bottom of the Cable Car Lift

When the cable car carrying Ar-Chee reached the top, a second cable car running on parallel lines, would descend to the bottom platform. That second car would take Ling Ting Tong, but not to the top. No, it would take him only about 15 feet off the ground where he would be trapped, suspended in the car along with No Quil's agent. Just hanging there until the Hong Kong Fire Department came to rescue him. With a nice, comfortable cage. A cage for his ride to the Hong Kong jail. From there he would be taken

* Beijing Ding-a-Ling: Mao of the CIA *

* A Fitting Finish *

back to Beijing to stand trial, along with Ar-Chee, for smuggling and selling drugs on the international market.

And Ling Ting Tong, unknown yet to him, would also face charges for assault with pointy quills. He would surely fire a quill or two at a fireman or a policeman when they put him into his cage and read him his rights.

Hong Kong Airport—90 Minutes Later

Luigi and Luisa's plan had worked to perfection. The whole capture had ended within seconds. When Ar-Chee stepped off the rising cable car, the net dropped. He began to fight and wrestle with it until he had trapped himself, completely enmeshed to the point that eventually the net would have to be cut out. There would be no way to unwrap the net.

Ling Ting Tong had backed into a corner of the cable car that had stopped too high above the ground for him to leap off. Mr. Ling scrambled from one corner of the cable car to the other, firing sharp quills at No Quil's agent, two firemen and a policeman who were trying to capture him and get him into a cage. Finally he had run out of quills by the time the firemen and policemen, dressed in rubber raincoats to protect them from being stuck, stuffed him into the cage for his ride to the hoosegow.

Luigi and Luisa had a good laugh seeing Ling Ting Tong without any quills. "He's not so fierce looking now," Luisa had said.

The Cats of the CIA and Cincinnati had given their statements to the local authorities and headed to the airport. There a U.S. State Department jet would pick them up and take them back to Beijing where another plane would head them toward Tokyo, and then home.

No Quil, the two agents he'd sent to Hong Kong yesterday, and Elwood would return to Beijing.

As planned, No Quil, assistant minister of porcupine catching, his agents and Elwood would take all the credit for capturing the big panda and the portly porcupine.

There would be no mention of four cats and a dancing pig from the United States.

And that's the way the President and Secretary of State—and Socks, too—wanted this adventure to end.

Epilogue
The Next Day

✱ Beijing Ding-a-Ling: Mao of the CIA ✱

In the Air Enroute to Tokyo

"Maybe we should have stayed for the big ceremony," Luigi said. "After all, it's not every day that a two-toed sloth, who also happens to be a friend of ours, is honored as a hero in his country."

Luisa said, "It's not every day that anybody even gives a thought to a sloth, no matter how many toes he or she may have."

She paused, and then sighed. "But I'm glad we're going home. We did our job, after all. Ar-Chee and Ling Ting Tong won't be smuggling any more opium for a long, long time."

Luigi looked at Buzzer Louis. "How long do you think that will be, big brother? How long will they be in jail in China do you think?"

Buzzer thought a moment, and then said, "I think it will be at least 20 years. Those two have created an international brouhaha. We've had to go to two countries--the Russian Federation and the People's Republic of China—just to rein them in. And sentences can be harsh in China, remember. So I think 15 to 20 years. And they'll be lucky if they're not sentenced to hard labor, too."

The U.S. State Department Gulfstream 650 had returned early this morning to Beijing's Capital Interntional Airport to pick up the Cats of the CIA and Cincinnati the dancing pig. Hu Jintao, China's premier, had declared today a national holiday in honor of Elwood the sloth. He would be presenting Elwood with the 1958 Great Leap Forward Medal, the country's highest

In the Air Enroute to Tokyo

award for patriotism and service to the people. That presentation would take place later today, and it would be carried worldwide by CNN and other international news channels.

Even though they were invited as special guests, Buzzer had declined. Socks would record the ceremony for her files. And for the Cats of the CIA and Cincinnati to see later.

"After all," Buzzer said, "we need to remain in the background, quietly doing our job. I made the premier promise not to mention anything about us. As a politician, he understands what might happen if certain people in Washington found out about us." He smiled at the kittens and added, "We can't have that. Not until Luigi runs for President. Right, Luigi?"

"Right, Buzzer!" Luigi stood and saluted. Months earlier, after their adventure in Italy, he had told POTUS that, one day, he would occupy the Oval Office as president.

Dusty Louise asked, "What about No Quil? Will he talk about us? And, even worse, what about No Way? And the worst yet, Elwood?"

Cincinnati said, "No Quil is basking in the glory of leading the effort to catch the porcupine Ling Ting Tong. He will be handsomely rewarded by his government. He'll probably even get a promotion. I spoke to him about it. He has nothing to gain by mentioning some cats and a pig from the United States."

Buzzer said, "As far as No Way is concerned... and his strange assistant, whatever her real name may be. They have agreed to never say anything. As if they never heard of Ling Ting Tong. If they do, Premier Hu Jintao has made it clear they would be sent to retraining. For a very, very long time."

"That leaves Elwood," Dusty said. "Can he keep quiet? He doesn't seem smart enough to understand the damage he could do by mentioning us. And certainly how bad it would be to tell all about us."

Luigi looked at Luisa. They smiled at one another. Then Luisa said, "Really, Dusty, who is going to believe Elwood, anyway? He may be a hero, but you've never tried to have a conversation with him like Luigi and I have. Whatever he may say—although we've told him not to talk—will be confusing, anyway. No, we're not going to worry about Elwood. Are we, Luigi?"

Luigi just shook his head. Then he asked, "Okay, what's the plan? Today, I mean? Where do we go from Tokyo? And how do we get there?"

Buzzer said, "Excellent questions, Luigi. We'll be in Tokyo in an hour. Let's get Socks on the line to see what plans she's made for us."

Luigi grabbed Buzzer's secure satellite phone and punched in Socks's number in the White House basement. They heard her phone ring twice before she answered.

"This is Socks. And you, my friends, are big heroes in the Oval Office this morning. Congratulations! Two more bad guys out of business. But even more important, you have helped POTUS make new progress in getting to know and working with two important heads of state. I'm talking about Vladimir Putin of the Russian Federation and Hu Jintao of the People's Republic of China."

Luigi stood up and saluted once again. "Don't forget Germany, France, Italy, Mexico, and Argentina, too, Socks. And that's all been in the last few months. We could be our own little United Nations."

Socks said, "I haven't forgotten, Luigi, and neither has the president. He wants you all to take some time off. Get some rest. For a rare change, there seems to be no pressing emergency anywhere in the world that he needs you to handle."

That's why we're calling, Socks," Buzzer said. "We know we're on our way to Tokyo. We'll be there in a few minutes. But what happens then? We don't have *The Flying Pig Machine* waiting for us there. So, how do we get back from Tokyo? And where is it we're going next?"

"Good questions, Buzzer. If you're all in agreement, here's what's about to happen. A State Department Gulfstream will meet you in Tokyo. It will take you first to the Hill Country Intergalactic Airport so all but Cincinnati can go straight home. The plane will change crews there and proceed with Cincinnati to Andrews Air Force Base here—just outside Washington, D.C. Cincinnati left his plane there. Remember? He'll go home from

* In the Air Enroute to Tokyo *

here. Or wherever he wants to go."

She added quickly, "On the flight from Tokyo to your home in the Texas Hill Country, POTUS and I will call you on the video-conference line. He wants a complete debriefing. Just tell him succinctly how you managed to capture the panda and the porcupine. And, of course, he wants to personally thank you for what you've just done. And, Luigi, for all the other things you've done over this summer. It has been, in his words, 'quite remarkable.'"

They all felt the plane slow and begin its descent into Tokyo. The captain confirmed what they anticipated. "We're beginning our descent into Tokyo. We'll be landing at Narita International Airport in about 20 minutes. Please buckle yourselves in. When we get there, another of our State Department planes will meet you to take you on to wherever you're going today. Have a safe flight."

Socks said, "I heard that. Buckle up, stay safe, and I'll talk to you when you get back home."

Luigi spoke up, "Wait! Socks, did you make any progress on that matter that Luisa and I asked you about two days ago? You know what I'm talking about?"

"Ah, yes, Luigi," Socks said. "Tell me, you two kittens, just how seriously did you think the President and Secretary of State would consider your request?"

Dusty Louise interrupted, "What are you two asking the president and Secretary of State for now?" she said. Clearly she was frightened at what mischief the twins might have stirred up at the very top of the U.S. government.

Socks came to their rescue. She said, "Dusty, don't be concerned. I had a little tete-a-tete with Luigi and Luisa. What they said made enough sense to me to take it forward to POTUS. The matter has been resolved. No problem."

"So," Luisa said, "What's the answer? Did the president agree with us? Or not?"

At that moment, their plane hit some turbulence and dropped rapidly. Buzzer's phone flew out of Luigi's paws, hit the ceiling, fell and rolled along the aisle."

A flight attendant picked it up, saw that it was still turned on,

* Beijing Ding-a-Ling: Mao of the CIA *

and shut it off. "Time to turn off all electronic devices," He said.

Before anybody could say anything, Luigi announced, "Luisa and I are not saying a word. Not one word. Don't even ask."

The twins crossed their front paws across their chests, stuck out their lower lips in a defiant look. And then they lost it. They began laughing hysterically.

The End
Until the Next Adventure of the Cats of the CIA

What's Next for the Cats of the CIA?

What did Luigi and Luisa ask Socks to talk to the President about?

Find out what these lovable crime fighters will be doing and where they will be going on their next adventure.

Check out the following pages for a brief excerpt from the next Cats of the CIA book . . .

Pharaohs' Follies
Kits of the CIA

By George Arnold

From Eakin Press
A Division of Wild Horse Media Group

Copyright © 2015, 2016 by George Arnold

Pharaohs' Follies
Kits of the CIA

Copyright © 2015, 2016 George Arnold

Introduction

Buzzer Louis and the cats of the CIA had been busy traveling the world catching bad guys for weeks, if not months. Mexico, Italy, Argentina, Brazil, France, Germany, Russia, and even China. Now they were enjoying some rest at Buzzer's little ranch in the Texas Hill Country.

After they returned from China last week and reported on their success in capturing Ar-Chee and Ling Ting Tong, the opium smuggling panda and portly porcupine, POTUS—President of the U.S.—had suggested they needed some time off.

Buzzer, a black-and-white tuxedo cat and retired director of operations of Cats In Action (DO/CIA) agreed. *I'm supposed to be retired*, he thought, *but all I've done for months now is chase international bad guys . . . all over the world. I'm ready for some time off.*

Dusty Louise, Buzzer's gray-tabby younger sister, was ready for a rest, too. While chasing the same bad guys, Dusty had learned to fly a twin-engine jet airplane. And she'd shared a lot of the piloting chores with their best friend Cincinnati the dancing pig. Cincinnati had owned a very nice twin-fanjet Sabreliner until the group was ready to leave China. As a joke, he'd suggested to the tiny orange tabby twins, Luisa and Luigi, that it would be nice to have a new Gulfstream 650. Bigger, faster, nicer—luxurious, even—the Gulfstream might just be every pilot's dream.

While Cincinnati had simply made an offhand remark to Luigi and Luisa, tiny orange tabby brother and sister twins of Buzzer and Dusty, the twins had taken him seriously. Without mention-

* Pharoahs' Follies: Kits of the CIA *

ing anything to him, they had created a compelling Power Point presentation for Socks, the head of Cats In Action in the White House basement. They listed all the advantages a new Gulfstream would provide for the missions of the CIA cats.

Luigi and Luisa had done such a good job with their presentation that Socks took it directly to POTUS and the Secretary of State, the only two officials in Washington who even knew of the existence of Cats In Action. Amazingly, both agreed that a larger, faster and more fuel-efficient plane would serve their common cause better.

So when Cincinnati the dancing pig got back to Washington and went to retrieve his former plane—*The Flying Pig Machine*—where he'd left it at Andrews Air Force Base, he found, instead, a brand new Gulfstream 650. The name painted on the fuselage under the pilot's window startled him. *Flying Pig Machine II* made his heart stop for a moment. *Can this be true?* he thought. *I just made a joke to Luigi and Luisa. Never gave it a second thought. Those two! They must have begged Socks. Even POTUS.*

Cincinnati's mind raced.

But he had no problem accepting the keys and title to the new plane. While Buzzer, Dusty Louise and Luigi and Luisa had returned to Buzzer's Texas ranch to rest, Cincinnati had stayed behind in Washington for a couple of days of instruction and flight hours in flying the new Gulfstream.

An experienced pilot in both planes and helicopters, he soon had mastered the Gulfstream. And he was quickly certified to fly it. He suspected someone at the White House had called the FAA—Federal Aviation Administration—and suggested they hurry up on his certification. But he didn't know for sure.

Now he had returned to his home base in Ohio to check on his business interests. Cincinnati owned 114 dance studios between Buffalo, New York, and Chicago, Illinois. Lately he'd been concerned that he hadn't been able to pay as much attention to them as he wanted to. But he found them operating well under the temporary direction of his British butler and right-hand man.

While the rest of the team wanted rest, Luigi and Luisa remained ready to start another adventure. They became bored

* Beijing Ding-a-Ling: Mao of the CIA *

with routine ranch life and, after several days of bugging the ranch manager, Dr. Buford Lewis, Ph.D. and Buford's very smart brother, Bogart-BOGART, both Labrador Retrievers, the kittens started calling Socks regularly, begging for another assignment. They didn't care where that assignment might lead them. They were ready to go.

Anywhere.

On the tenth day after their return from China, Socks finally did call. Luigi had answered the phone. Seeing it was Socks on the line, he punched up speaker-phone and sent Luisa scurrying to get Buzzer and Dusty.

"Hello. This is Buzzer's Ranch," Luigi said, "where every phone call ends in a secret mission." He laughed, and then said, "Hello, Socks. What have you got for us today?"

"Luigi," Socks said, "can Buzzer, Dusty and Luisa hear me?"

"They're here, Socks. Go ahead," Luigi said.

"I'm coming to visit all of you in the morning," Socks said.

"You're coming here?" Luisa blurted out. "You've never been here before."

Socks said, "There's a first time for everything, Luisa. And I'm bringing a special guest. Cincinnati's picking us up very early tomorrow in his new plane. We should be the Hill Country Intergalactic Airport before noon."

Buzzer said, "I'll have Dr. Lewis and Bogart-BOGART pick you up in our truck."

"That won't be necessary, Buzzer," Socks said. "We'll be met by a small team from San Antonio. They won't be coming into your house, though. They'll stand by outside."

Dusty's well-known curiosity got the best of her. "Okay, Socks. What's going on? Why all the mystery? Who's coming with you and Cincinnati? And why are you coming here?"

Socks answered, "Right, Dusty, let me take those questions one at a time.

"Why all the mystery? Because the trip is top secret.

"Who is coming with me? That's a need-to-know answer. And you don't need to know until tomorrow. National security, you see.

* Pharoahs' Follies: Kits of the CIA *

"And why am I coming there? The answer's the same. And here it is: I have a new assignment for you. But it must be discussed in absolute isolation. We'll use your house. The FBI will sweep it for listening devices—bugs, we call them—in the morning before we get there.

"Does that answer your questions?" Socks said.

"All but two," Luigi said. "Where are we going? And what will we be doing there?"

Luisa piped up, "We like to be prepared, you know, Socks. And we'll have time to be really prepared if we at least have a location to research."

Socks said, "I'll text you some clues. If you can figure them out, you'll have all evening and most of tomorrow morning to do your research. How's that?"

Before the twins could answer, Dusty interrupted. "Is Cincinnati on the line?" she asked.

"I'm here," the dancing pig said.

"Okay, Cincinnati," Dusty said. "Once we figure out the location, do you want me to find refueling stops along the way?"

"Not necessary," the dancing pig said. "We'll leave from Washington. D.C., and this new plane has a range of 8,000 miles. No need to stop."

"Am I still going to be your co-pilot?" Dusty said, hoping to keep going with her flying lessons.

"Sure," Cincinnati answered. "I'll have to teach you about the new plane. It's nifty. You're going to love it."

Socks said, "Are we finished now? We'll see you before noon tomorrow."

"Wait! Luigi shouted. "Text us the clues."

"I'm doing that right now," Socks said as she ended the call.

At once, Buzzer's secure satellite phone jingled. Socks's text had come through.

Buzzer began to read the clues. "First clue," he said. *"There's a lot of sand. More sand than you can imagine."*

"Go on" Luisa said. "That could be lots of places."

"Second clue. *There's a long, long river.*"

"One more clue" Luigi said.

Buzzer read on. *"There are famous old buildings with four sides. But they're pointed at their tops."*

"Egypt!" Luigi and Luisa shouted in unison.

"We're going to Egypt," Luigi continued.

"Now all we need to know is why," Dusty Louise said. But the twins didn't hear her. They had raced pell-mell to their computer to begin checking out Egypt.

Dusty shook her head. "By tomorrow morning," she said, "they will know more about Egypt than Egyptian historians."

Thanks to Those Who Helped

If anyone should ever tell you that they wrote a book alone, without help, you can bet two things: first, the book is likely not worth reading; and that writer is a protective control freak. In all of my books, you will find acknowledgments of dozens of individuals who played a significant role in making the story and the writing better than it would have been without their participation.

Via email, I recruit a panel of readers—manuscript readers. These brave and adventurous literary souls go through up to 20 weeks of activity, reading two draft chapters each week and reacting to those drafts with corrections and suggestions. And, yes, I do pay careful attention to their suggestions. Otherwise, why ask them? Besides, readers often have better ideas than I, anyway.

At the end of this manuscript-reading cycle, I ask each of them to complete and submit their answers to a questionnaire. It's usually about 20 questions long, most of them semantic differential questions (like hot-cold, beautiful-ugly), plus a few open-ended opportunities to wax philosophical . . . and to tell me in their own words what they really think.

What's in the participation process for these intrepid readers? Not much, really. The personal satisfaction of helping birth a new book we can all take pride in; credit for their invaluable help in the book itself; and a personalized, signed copy of the finished book from the first press run.

I didn't invent the idea of reader panels. In the world of marketing, which I inhabited for thirty-plus career years, it's called *In-Home Placement Testing*. Savvy marketers use it all the time to help not only define and refine the attributes of their products, but also to identify primary targets, unique selling points, even the effectiveness of verbal and written descriptions.

Now that you know more than you ever cared to know about manuscript testing, I want to pass along a million thanks to the following individuals whose critical efforts improved this book immensely:

Student Readers

Irvine, California
   Mariel Clark — High School Student
   Julianne Clark — Sixth Grade Student

Adult Readers

Seattle, Washington
   Marion Woodfield — Retired Advertising Executive

Los Angeles, California
   Betty Cao — Mandarin Translator, Marketer

Irvine, California
   Margery Arnold, Ph.D. — Child Psychologist

Georgetown, Texas
   Connie Carden — Retired Teacher

San Antonio, Texas
   Ken Squier — Author, Entrepreneur

Houston, Texas
   Julie B. Fix, APR — Assistant Professor, University of Houston; Fellow, Public Relations Society of America

St. Petersburg, Florida
   James Arnold — Retired United Airlines Captain
   Barbara Arnold — Grandmother and Sailor

Boston, Massachusetts
   Jason Eckhardt — Political Cartoonist, Illustrator

Navasota, Texas
   Mike Cooper — Author, Martial Arts Teacher

Dallas/Fort Worth, Texas
   Edward Stone — Chairman Emeritus, The Dallas Marketing Group
   Mary Arnold — Retired Landscape Horticulturist
   Marilyn Pippin, APR — President, Hopkins Public Relations
   Don Ward — Retired Marketing Executive
   Cynthia Voliva — Youth Minister

My Publisher—Wild Horse Media Group

Relationships between authors and publishers are intimate, yet distant. And I think that's how it should be. I love my publisher. Eakin Press is now a division of Wild Horse Media Group, one of the largest independent presses in the South/Southwest. Billy Huckaby, who heads up the whole magilla, is a pleasure to work with. He does his job. I do mine. We have very little contact (or need for contact) until a manuscript is ready (not finished. "Finished manuscript" is an oxymoron). Then we have a brief meeting. I give him an electronic file. We discuss a production schedule. Then we both go back to doing what we do. Separately. Trying to make one another a little money by informing, entertaining and raising an occasional relevant social issue for discussion.

Thank you, Billy. It's fun to work with you.

My Retail Partners and Supporters

During the past dozen or so years, I have developed close working relationships with Community Relations Managers at Barnes & Noble Booksellers, mostly in Texas. You know who you are—in Dallas/Fort Worth, Houston, Austin and San Antonio. Thank you. I'm grateful for your continued support of my efforts. Together, we conduct about two dozen in-store signing events every year. Most of them are three-day weekends. It's our goal, not only to introduce and sell a lot of books, but also to make friends for the store and the author , and to support the Barnes & Noble brand.

I also very much appreciate both the support of and the plight facing independent book retailers today. Thank you for ordering and selling my books.

Finally, to You—My Readers

Without readers, of course, there would be no need for authors or booksellers. It takes time, but over the years, I have developed a following of fans who actually look forward to the next book I'm writing. I love you all. As long as I'm able, I plan to produce two books a year—a Cats of the CIA adventure, and another fiction novel to be determined.

Obligatory Mea Culpa

Members of my reader panel, my publisher and I try uncommonly hard to be sure our facts are accurate, our spelling and grammar are pluperfect, pages are numbered correctly, and the product is what it should be—error free.

If you should find mistakes in this book, they are my responsibility, and mine, alone. The buck stops with me.

George Arnold
Dallas/Fort Worth, Texas
2015

Glossary

Pronunciation Guide to Common Mandarin Words and Phrases

English	Mandarin	Say it Like This
A		
Afternoon	下午	Xia\ wu^
Airplane	飞机	Fei- ji-
Airport	飞机场	Fei- ji- chang^
American Express	美国运通	Mei^ guo/ yun\ tong-
Ankle	脚裸	Jiao^ huai/
Apples	苹果	Ping/ guo^
April	四月	Si\ yue\
Arm	手臂	Shou^ bi\
August	八月	Ba- yue\
Aunt	姨妈	Yi/ ma-
B		
Bananas	香蕉	Xiang- jiao-
Bank	银行	Yin/ hang/
Bathroom	浴室	Yu\ shi\
Beans	豆	Dou\
Bed	床	Chuang/
Beijing	北京	Bei^ jing-
Bellman	行李员	Xing/ li^yuan/
Belt	皮带	Pi/ dai\
Bicycle	自行车	Zi\ xing/ che-
Billion	十亿	Shi/ yi\
Bird	鸟	Niao^
Black	黑色	Hei- se\

* Glossary *

Blouse	女式衬衣	Nv^shi\ chen\ yi-
Blue	蓝色	Lan/ se\
Boat	船	Chuan/
Boots	靴子	Xue- zi
Bowl	碗	Wan^
Bread	面包	Mian\ bao-
Brother	兄弟	Xiong- di\
Brown	棕色	Zhong- se\
Bus	公车	Gong- che-
Butter	牛油	Niu/ you/
C		
Cab	出租车	Chu- zu- che-
Cab driver	出租车司机	Chu- zu- che- si- ji
Camel	骆驼	Luo\ tuo/
Cake	蛋糕	Dan\ gao-
Cap	帽子	Mao\ zi
Car	小轿车	Xiao^ jiao\ che
Carrots	萝卜	Luo/ bo
Cat	猫	Mao-
Cereal	谷类物	Gu^lei\ wu\
Chair	椅子	Yi^ zi
Change	改变	Gai^ bian\
Check in	登记入住	Deng- ji\ ru\ zhu\
Check out	退房	Tui\fang/
Chest	胸部	Xiong- bu\
Chicken	鸡	Ji-
Chin	下巴	Xia\ ba
Chocolate	巧克力	Qiao^ ke li\
Chopsticks	筷子	Kuai\ zi

Coat	大衣	Da\ yi
Coins	银币	Yin/ bi\
Cloudy	多云的	Duo- yun/ de
Cold	冷	Leng^
Coffee shop	咖啡店	Ka- fei- dian\
Concierge	礼宾部	Li^ bin- bu\
Cookies	饼干	Bing^ gan-
Corn	玉米	Yu\ mi^
Cost	成本	Cheng/ ben^
Cow	奶牛	Nai^ niu/
Cream	奶油	Nai^ you/
Credit card	信用卡	Xin\ yong\ ka^
Cucumbers	青瓜	Qing- gua-
Cup	杯子	Bei- zi
D		
Dark	黑暗的	Hei-an\ de
Day	白天	Bai/ tian-
December	十二月	Shi/ er\ yue\
Desk clerk	前台服务员	Qian/ tai/ fu/wu\ yuan/
Discover	发现	Fa- xian\
Doctor	医生	Yi- sheng-
Dog	狗	Gou^
Dollars	美金	Mei^jin-
Donut	甜甜圈	Tian/ tian/ quan/
Duck	鸭子	Ya- zi
E		
Ear	耳朵	Er^ duo
Eight	八	Ba

* Glossary *

Eighty	八十	Ba- shi/
Elbow	手肘	Shou^ zhou^
Elephant	大象	Da\ xiang\
Elevator	升降机	Sheng- jiang\ ji-
Evening	晚上	Wan^ shang\
Exchange rate	汇率	Hui\ lv\
Excuse me	打扰了	Da^ rao^ le
Eye	眼睛	Yan^ jing-
F		
Fall	秋天	Qiu- tian-
Father	爸爸	Ba\ ba\
February	二月	Er\ yue\
Female cousin	堂姐妹	Tang/ jie^ mei\
Fifty	五十	Wu^ shi/
Fingers	手指	Shou/ zhi^
Five	五	Wu^
Fish	鱼	Yu/
Flight	飞机	Fei- ji-
Foot	脚	Jiao^
Fork	叉子	Cha- zi
Forty	四十	Si\ shi/
Four	四	Si\
Friday	星期五	Xing- qi- wu^
G		
Galoshes	胶鞋	Jiao- xie/
Gate	大门	Da\ men/
Glass	玻璃杯	Bo- li bei-
Gloves	手套	Shou^ tao\

Goat	山羊	Shan- yang/
Gold	金	Jin-
Goodbye	再见	Zai\ jian\
Grandfather	祖父亲	Zu^ fu\ qin-
Grandmother	祖母亲	Zu^ mu^ qin-
Gray	黑色	Hei- se\
Great Wall	长城	Chang/ cheng/
Green	绿色	Lv\ se\
Guide	指南	Zhi^ nan/

H

Hail	冰雹	Bing- bao/
Hair	头发	Tou/ fa
Hand	手	Shou^
Hat	帽子	Mao\ zi
Head	头	Tou/
Heart	心脏	Xin- zang\
Hip	臀部	Tun/ bu\
Horse	马	Ma^
Hospital	医院	Yi- yuan\
Hot	热	Re\
Hotel	酒店	Jiu^ dian\
Hundred	百	Babi^

I-J-K

Ice cream	雪糕	Xue^ gao-
Jacket	外套	Wai\ tao\
January	一月	Yi- yue\
July	7月	Qi- yue\
June	六月	Liu\ yue\

* Glossary *

Knee	膝盖	xi- gai\
Knife	刀子	Dao\ zi
L		
Leg	脚	Jiao^
Lemon	柠檬	Ning/ meng
Lettuce	生菜	Sheng- chai\
Light	灯	Deng-
Limousine	豪华轿车	Hao/ hua/ jiao\ che -
Lion	狮子	Shi- zi
Luggage	行李	Xing/ li^
M		
Male cousin	表/堂兄	Biao^ tang/ xiong-
March	三月	San- yue\
MasterCard	万事达卡	Wan\ shi\ da/
May	五月	Wu^ yue\
Meat	肉	Rou\
Menu	菜谱	Cai\ pu^
Midnight	午夜	Wu^ ye\
Million	百万	Bai^ wan\
Milk	牛奶	Niu/ nai^
Mittens	毛线手套	Mao/ rong/ shou^ tao\
Monday	星期一	Xing- qi yi-
Money	钱	Qian/
Monkey	猴子	Hou/ zi
Month	月份	Yue\ fen\
Moon	月	Yue\
Morning	早上	Zao^ shang\

Mother	母亲	Mu^ qin-
Museum	博物馆	Bo/ wu\ guan^

N-O

Napkin	餐巾	Can- jin-
Neapolitan	三色雪糕	San- se\ xue^ gao-
Neck	颈部	Jing^ bu\
Night	夜晚	Ye\ wan^
Nine	九	Jiu^
Ninety	九十	Jiu^ shi/
Noodles	面条	Mian\ tiao/
Noon	中午	Zhong- wu^
Nose	鼻子	Bi/ zi
November	十一月	Shi/ yi yue\
Nurse	护士	Hu\ shi\
October	十月	Shi/ yue\
One	一	Yi-
Orange	橙子	Cheng/ zi
Orange juice	橙子汁	Cheng/ zi zhi-

P-Q

Palace	宫殿	Gong- dian\
Panda	熊猫	Xiong/ mao-
Pants	裤子	Ku\ zi
Parka		Da\ yi-
Peach	桃子	Tao/ zi
Peas	豌豆	Wan- dou \
Pepper	胡椒	Hu/ jiao-
Pharmacist	药剂师	Yao\ ji- shi-
Pig	猪	Zhu-

* Glossary *

Pillow	枕头	Zhen^ tou/
Pilot	飞行员	Fei- xing/ yuan/
Pink	粉红色	Fen^ hong/ se\
Pistachio	开心果	Kai- xin- guo^
Plate	碟子	Die/ zi
Policeman	警察	Jing^ cha/
Porcupine	箭猪	Jian\ zhu-
Pork	猪肉	Zhu- rou\
Price	价格	Jia\ ge/
Puma	美洲狮	Mei^ zhou- shi-
Purple	紫色	Zi^ se\
Quill	鹅毛笔	E/ MAO/ BI^
R		
Rain	下雨	Xia\ yu^
Raincoat	雨衣	Yu^ yi
Rainy	下雨天	Xia\ yu^ tian-
Raspberry		Fu\ pan/ zi
Red	红色	Hong/ se\
Restaurant	餐馆	Can- guan-
Rickshaw	人力车	Ren/ li\ che-
Room	房间	Fang- jian-
Room service	客房服务	Ke\ fang/ fu/ wu\
S		
Salt	盐	Yan/
Saturday	星期六	Xing- qi- liu\
Saucer	茶杯碟	Cha/ bei-die/
September	九月	Jiu^ yue\
Season	季节	Ji\ jie/

* Beijing Ding-a-Ling: Mao of the CIA *

Seven	七	Qi-
Seventy	七十	Qi- shi/
Sheep	绵羊	Mian/ yang/
Sheet	床单	Chuang/ dan-
Shirt	衬衣	Chen\ yi
Shoes	鞋子	Xie/ zi
Shopkeeper	店主	Dian\ zhu^
Shuttle	穿梭巴士	Chuan-shuo- ba- shi\
Shoulder	肩膀	Jian- bang^
Sidewalk	行人路	Xing/ren/ lu\
Silver	银色	Yin/ se\
Sister	姐妹	Jie^ mei\
Six	六	Liu\
Sixty	六十	Liu\ shi/
Ship	船	Chuan/
Shin	小腿	Xiao^ tui^
skirt	裙子	Qun/ zi
Sleet	袖子	Xiu\ zi
Sloth	树懒	Shu\ lan^
Slip	背心睡衣	Bei\ xin- shui\ yi
Socks	袜子	Wa\ zi
Snake	蛇	She/
Snow	下雪	Xia\ xue^
Sorry	对不起	Dui\ bu\ qi^
Soup	汤	Tang-
Spoon	汤匙	Tang- shi/
Spring	春天	Chun- tian-
Stomach	胃	Wei\
Stormy	暴风雨的	Bao\ feng\ yu^

* Glossary *

Strawberry	草莓	Cao^ mei/
Sugar	糖	Tang/
Suite	套房	Tao\ fang/
Sun	太阳	Tai\ yang/
Sundown	黄昏	Huang/ hun-
Sunday	星期天	Xing- qi- tian-
Sunshine	阳光的	Yang/ guang- de
Sunup	日出	Ri\ chu-
Summer	夏天	Xia\ tian-
Sweater	毛衣	Mao- yi-
T		
Table	桌子	Zhuo- zi
Tablecloth	桌布	Zhuo- bu\
Tan	黝黑色	You^ hei- se\
Taxi	出租车	Chu-zu- che
Temperature	温度	Wen- du\
Thigh	大腿	Da\ tui^
Tiger	老虎	Lao/ hu^
Thirty	三十	San- shi/
Thousand	千	Qian-
Three	三	San-
Thursday	星期四	Xing-qi- si\
Today	今天	Jin- tian-
Toe	脚趾	Jiao^zhi^
Towel	毛巾	Mao/ jin-
Train	火车	Huo^ che
Traveler's checks	旅行支票	Lv^ xing/ zhi- piao\
Twenty	二十	Er\ shi/
Two	二	Er\

U-V-W		
Umbrella	雨伞	Yu^ san^
Uncle	叔伯	Shu- bo/
Vanilla	香草味	Xiang- cao^wei\
Visa	签证	Qian- zheng\
Waitperson	侍应	Shi\ ying\
Walking	走路	Zou^ lu\
Week	星期	Xing- qi
Weather	天气	Tian- qi\
White	白色	Bai/ se\
Wind	风	Feng-
Winter	冬天	Dong- tian-
Wolf	狼	Lang/
Wrist	手腕	Shou^ wan/
X-Y-Z		
Yellow	黄色	Huang/ se\
Yuan Renminbi	人民币	Ren/ min/ bi\
Zero	零	Ling/

Other Books by the Author
Adult Fiction – Detective Craig Rylander Clover-Mysteries By Arnold and Squier

- **ENIGMA:** *A Mystery:* Seven young girls have disappeared from the streets of Austin, Texas, presumably kidnapped by "The Austin Monster," leaving no clues, no trace. APD Detective Sergeant Craig Rylander and Family and Protective Services Psychologist Dr. Amy Clark race against time to find the girls. Will Craig–with his no-nonsense style of catching criminals–and Amy--with her in-depth understanding of the violent criminal mind–find the girls in time? And, if they do find them, will they be alive? Dead? Or something in between? The clock is ticking.

- **UNDERCURRENTS:** *The Van Pelt Enigma:* Craig and Amy begin what they think is an investigation of two local cases–an arson murder and a terrorist-like car bombing–only to step unwittingly into an international terrorist ring dating back more than two-hundred years. A ring controlled by the descendants of the Romanoff family, Russia's last Czars. They, along with the FBI, Texas Rangers, Interpol and the CIA, wander perilously into the crosshairs of the assassins themselves. Will Craig and his team solve the arson and car bombing without becoming victims of assassination? Extraordinary measures are called for.

- **CONFLICTION:** *A Moral Enigma:* Disappointed in the criminal justice system that somehow can't shut down a ring of international assassins after two-hundred years, Austin Police Detective Sergeant Craig Rylander accepts a leave-of-absence from APD and takes on a privately-financed worldwide hunt to put an end to the assassins himself. Amply financed and furnished with fake identifications and a "black" Gulfstream G-550 airplane, will Craig and his small team--a rookie detective from Tucson and an old, mysterious Navajo shaman and tracker--find the elusive and dangerous Felix Pavlovich, head of the *Czarists*? Or will Pavlovich and his group of international assassins kill Craig and his team first?

- **ADVENTURES OF THE CHURCH-LADY GANG:** *A Conspiracy of Crones:* Bedeviled and threatened for an entire year with strange cases involving child abusers, domestic vigilante groups and a ring of international assassins, APD Detective Sergeant Craig Rylander gets himself assigned to a case he thinks will be simpler and provide a bit of a breather–a local gang of eccentric Robin Hood wannabe church ladies. Stereotypical church ladies banded together to help the less fortunate by hook or by crook. Occasionally by crook. If Craig thought tracking down, all over the world, a 200-year-old assassination organization would be the kind of case to try his patience, threaten his life and his often brilliant deductive reasoning powers, he badly underestimated the Church Ladies. No scam is too bizarre for this pious little group, as Craig and his team will quickly learn. Warm, human and funny to the bone, **ADVENTURES OF THE CHURCH LADY GANG** presents a hilarious puzzle for Craig to unravel. To Craig, Dominus vobiscum, and to Craig's entire team, Et cum spiritu tuo.

- **FIRE AND ICE: BEYOND ALCHEMY,** *by George Arnold* Over three or four billion years, a basketball-sized mass weighing more than 4,800 pounds has drifted upward from the earth's molten center . . . through the mantle and the crust to rest, at last, near the surface on the Central Siberian Plateau, seven degrees north of the Arctic Circle. The U.S. Central Intelligence Agency has confirmed the mass is pure Plutonium. Enough to fuel more than 100 nuclear bombs. But who else knows? Monica Skrabacz, head of the Russian desk at Langley, implores Craig Rylander to form a team to recover the geological aberration that could be used to destroy civilization as we know it. Based on past experience, she trusts only Craig for this mission. Based on his own past experience, he doesn't trust Monica, period. But the stakes are high. Too high to ignore. Will he accept the assignment? And if he does, will his team recover the Plutonium before it falls into the hands of terrorists? Or nationalist despots desperate to have "The Bomb"? Hundreds of ticking dirty-suitcase bombs and dozens of big bombs are counting down.

- **COMING 2016: MULLIGAN:** *Justice Reclaimed by George Arnold* What happens when a murder investigation goes off the rails and a young woman is convicted of second-degree murder when evidence is lacking and her attorney has never before tried a criminal case? Rosa Salinas, found guilty by an Austin, Texas jury, immediately receives a *mulligan* from Judge Susan Bronson, who calls the trial a "circus." The judge orders a new investigation, and the job falls to Detective Lt. Craig Rylander and his team. They confront a belligerent local sheriff, tight-lipped witnesses, and an on-going series of felonies. Will they be able to figure out who the murderer really was? Or might it have been Rosa Salinas all along? From an isolated West Texas ranch to a Mexican whorehouse, Detectives Gady Esparza and Tom Sellers, and ADA Sydney Reynolds are determined to reclaim justice.

Nonfiction for Readers of all Ages – by George Arnold

- *Growing Up Simple: An Irreverent Look at Kids in the 1950s:* With foreword by Texas icon Liz Carpenter, this multi-award winner has been compared favorably by critics to Tom Sawyer. Winner of the IPPY (Independent Publishers' Association) humor award as the funniest book published in North America in 2003; the Violet Crown Award from Barnes & Noble as the best nonfiction book of 2003 by a Texas author; and a coveted Silver Spur, Growing Up Simple explores the lives of a merry band of overachievers bent on saving the world from itself in the 1950s. Must-read for anyone born between 1939 and 1947–the "In-Betweeners." And for anybody else who enjoys nonstop belly laughs.

- *Chick Magnates, Ayatollean Televangelist, & A Pig Farmer's Beef: Inside the Sometimes Hilarious World of Advertising:* Funny to the bone–both human and chicken–Chick Magnates reports on the world of advertising agencies and their clients during the last quarter of the 20th century, taking names and kicking butt with a series of chronological vignettes that are totally true, but almost unbelievable. It's a tribute to creative thinking down through civilized history—thinking and action that have raised us all out of cave-dwelling and rubbing sticks together to make fire.

- *BestSeller: Must-Read Author's Guide to Successfully Selling Your Book:* The truth, the whole truth, and nothing but the truth about the author's role in the marketing of his or her own books, this book inspires and sometimes frightens would-be authors. Accompanied by free 90-minute workshops in bookstores for writers who want to be published and published authors who

Cats of the C.I.A. Fiction Series for Readers from 8 to 108 by George Arnold

- *Get Fred-X: The Cats of the C.I.A. (English only):* Meet Buzzer Louis, black-and-white tuxedo cat and retired director of operations of the C.I.A.–Cats in Action–a secret group of enforcers run out of the White House basement by a gray tabby named Socks. Buzzer, his gray-tabby sister, Dusty Louise, their hilarious tiny orange tabby twin siblings, Luigi and Luisa, and Buzzer's best friend and former contract operative, Cincinnati the dancing pig, introduce this fun and educational series by tracking down the infamous international catnapper, Fred-X, a giant owl who grabs cats and tries to fly them nightly to Memphis.

- *Hunt for Fred-X: Los Gatos of the C.I.A. (English/elementary Spanish):* Buzzer Louis, Dusty Louise, Luigi and Luisa, and Cincinnati the dancing pig head to Mexico at the request of the Mexican president to help the *Federales* (Mexican national police) stop the catnapping Fred-X from grabbing cats in *Chihuahua* and flying them to the *Yucatán* to sell into slavery in Aruba. Along the way, they learn to speak considerable Mexican Spanish. You will, too, with a 750-word and -phrase vocabulary and pronunciation guide in Spanish as spoken in Mexico.

- *Fred-X Rising: I Gatti of the C.I.A. (English/elementary Italian):* Our crime-fighting cats and Cincinnati are summoned to Italy by Buzzer's first cousin, Césare Pepperoni Giaccomazza, head of the Rome bureau of Interpol, to again capture Fred-X, who this time has the help of his German girlfriend, Frieda-K, and a greedy cardinal from the Vatican, capturing Italian cats to take to a one-armed ship's captain in Venice who plans to transport them in his old rust-bucket ship to the cat slave trade in Tunisia. As they track down the catnapping owl, they learn considerable Italian. You will, too, with a 750-word and -phrase vocabulary and pronunciation guide in Italian as spoken in Italy.

- *Tango With a Puma: Los Gatos of the C.I.A. (English/intermediate Spanish):* Fresh from capturing Fred-X in Italy, our heroes are invited to Argentina to help the PFA (*Policia Federal de Argentina*) capture the infamous international terrorist, Carlos the puma, just escaped from a maximum security prison at the headwaters of the Amazon River and headed for Buenos Aires. This time a diabolical, but simple, plan by Luigi and Luisa to corral the ingenious big cat in *Los Jardines de Palermo*, a big park in the Argentinean capital, Buenos Aires. In the process, they polish up and expand their Spanish. You will, too, with a 750-word and -phrase vocabulary and pronunciation guide in more formal, intermediate Spanish as spoken in Argentina.

- *Eiffel's Trifles & Troubles: Les Chats of the C.I.A. (English/elementary French)*: When Carlos the puma again escapes from the headquarters of the PFA in Buenos Aires, Socks' spy satellite intercepts a phone call to his headquarters from Carlos on a ship in the South Atlantic. He's headed for Paris, and so are our heroes. Again they lay a clever plan to capture Carlos once and for all–even while touring the sites and sights of Paris, the City of Lights. And they learn to speak considerable French along the way. You will, too, with a 750-word and -phrase vocabulary and pronunciation guide in basic French as spoken in Paris.

- *München Madness: Die Katzen of the C.I.A. (English/elementary German)*: The Bavarian region around Munich is the setting for the final attempt to capture Carlos the puma and return him to the authorities in Argentina, where's he still wanted as a fugitive and for bombing the headquarters of the national police, the PFA–*Policia Federal de Argentina*. As they track Carlos in Bavaria, they learn to speak considerable German. You will, too, with a 750-word and -phrase vocabulary and pronunciation guide in basic German as spoken in Germany.

- *Kremlin Kerfuffle: Koshki of the C.I.A. (English/elementary Russian)*: Fresh from their Bavarian adventure tracking down Carlos the puma, the cats of the C.I.A. and Cincinnati the dancing pig are commanded secretly by the U.S. President (POTUS) to travel once again, this time to Russia. Their mission: capture the infamous international opium smuggler from Beijing, Ar-Chee the panda. Ar-Chee, you see, is the world's most active smuggler of opium from the poppy fields of Afghanistan via secret routes through the People's Republic of China, and he's set his sights on the lucrative Moscow market. POTUS and Russia's president, meeting in secret in Iceland, are determined, rather than sending in the troops, to cut off Ar-Chee's supply lines by simply capturing the big panda as he plies his trade around the Kremlin. Along the way, our heroes learn to speak considerable Russian. You will, too, with a 750-word and –phrase vocabulary and pronunciation guide in Russian as spoken in Moscow.

- *Beijing Ding-a-Ling: Mao of the C.I.A.:* The President of the United States, at the request of the Premier of the People's Republic of China, dispatches Buzzer Louis and the Cats of the CIA to help track down the brains behind Ar-Chee's opium smuggling ring. You see, Ling Ting Tong, a brilliant, multi-lingual porcupine, is known to be hiding in the Chinese capital. Having captured Mr. Ling's front man, Ar-Chee the panda, in Moscow, it's now up to the clandestine CIA cats to find Ling Ting Tong and put an end to the smuggling of opium from Afghanistan for resale along the Pacific Rim and in Moscow. Join the lovable twins, Luigi and Luisa, their brother and sister, Buzzer Louis and Dusty Louise, as they track down the porcupine with the help of their cohort, Cincinnati the dancing pig. The whole team learns to speak some Mandarin. So will you with the 750-word and –phrase vocabulary and pronunciation guide built right into the story.

- **COMING SOON:** *Pharaohs' Follies: Kits of the CIA.* The understanding and scientific manipulation of DNA have apparently led to a secret and diabolic experiment among a group of rogue scientists. Working clandestinely in the Egyptian desert, this group is determined to clone a new race of Pharaohs . . . with DNA from the 5,000 year-old bones of ancient pharaohs stolen from the pyramids. Who better to locate the base of these experiments and bring the whole misguided effort to a halt than the equally clandestine Cats of the CIA? Dispatched to Egypt by POTUS, President of the United States, our clever and lovable international detectives face a mission that's both dangerous and historically educational. Amongst the pyramids of the Nile Valley, they learn to speak considerable Arabic. You will, too, with a 750-word and –phrase vocabulary and pronunciation guide in Arabic built right into the story.

About the Author

Beijing Ding-a-Ling is George's 17th book from Eakin Press since 2002 . . . and the eighth in the Cats of the CIA set. Previous CIA Cats' books have included both elementary and intermediate Spanish (Mexico and Argentina, respectively), Italian (the Trentino Alps), French (Paris), German (München), and Russian (Moscow).

The four cats—Buzzer Louis, Dusty Louise, Luigi and Luisa—are real. They live with George's family in the Dallas/Fort Worth area. If you were to ask them, however, they would quickly tell you that George and Mary, his wife of 50 years, live at *their* house. Like cats everywhere, the Cats of the CIA are masters of their domain, wherever that may be.

George explains why he decided, some 10 years ago, to begin writing semi-bilingual international adventures. "I have been lucky enough," he said, "to travel to many parts of the world, including almost every country in which the books are set. For *Beijing Ding-a-Ling*, I spent 27 days in the People's Republic of China. And everywhere in my travels, I've seen small children (and adults, of course) speaking multiple languages.

"From the cradle."

He continued, "But not in the U.S. We tend not to introduce other languages in our education systems until middle school—or later. But an infant's mind is sponge-like. Learning multiple languages, along with one's own country's language, is just easier for a small child. So I decided to see if I could pique the reading world's interest in not only other languages, but also other countries and cultures.

"The cats at our house have given me that platform. My own little soapbox," he said.

In addition to the CIA Cats' books, George has written two highly-awarded non-fiction novels, a how-to book for writers wanting to be published and for published authors wanting to sell 20 times as many books. With old friend and co-author Ken Squier, he has written five fictional detective novels, all starring Austin, Texas, police detective Craig Rylander.

George and Mary have four children and seven grandchildren. They live in The Dallas/Fort Worth Metroplex.

See more at George's Website: www.CIAcats.com

CPSIA information can be obtained
at www.ICGtesting.com
Printed in the USA
LVHW05s1616041018
592411LV00011B/1047/P

9 781681 790206